THEODORE TAYLOR

THE
CHILDREN'S
WAR

Doubleday & Company, Inc.

GARDEN CITY, NEW YORK

Library of Congress Catalog Card Number 73–144304.
Copyright © 1971 by Theodore Taylor. All Rights
Reserved. Printed in the United States of America.
First Edition.

CONTENTS

Part I   THE GUN   11

Part II   THE TEACHER   63

Part III   THE INVADERS   107

THE CHILDREN'S WAR

Part I

THE GUN

[1]

June 5, 1941: I remember it was very foggy when I awakened about five-thirty. Our settlement, a lonely scattering of frame and log houses tucked beneath two ridges facing the beach, was wrapped in grayness. That happened often during summer in Alaska, although the sun would be shining brightly on the wide, barren plain behind us. It hardly set at all in June, staying in the sky endlessly like a great round gold bird without wings.

I ran across the cold linoleum floor straight to the kitchen. I was certain what was out there. Sure enough, it was standing up in my chair. My father, Chief Jacob Scofield, already dressed in his Navy uniform to go over to Unigak Island, was by it, watching my face for reaction.

There it was, all right, a shining .410 gauge shotgun, so beautiful I closed my eyes and opened them again. Blue barrel, gleaming dark stock, and beside it, in the seat, a box of Remington shells. I had wanted it since I was ten.

"You be careful with that," my mother said. She thought I was still too young for it.

"That's a beginner's gun," my father said, a satisfied grin on his face. I'd been hunting and fishing with him since I was five or six. He'd taught me much about guns already, and I'd fired his twelve gauge when I was only seven.

"Only way to know is by doin'," he added.

My mother, a plump soft-skinned woman with gold-rimmed glasses and honey hair that was beginning to show some gray strands, had a brother who was maimed in a hunting accident back in Tennessee. So she always worried more than she should have.

My father had been around guns all his life. He was born deep in the Blue Ridge Mountains of North Carolina and had held a gun before he'd ever seen an automobile. At least, he'd said that.

"You go up the plain, Dory, or up the river, way up, when you fire that thing," my mother said, her face not at all happy.

"Cece, you think he's gonna shoot up the settlement? He knows better'n that." A rawboned man, well over six feet, with a craggy mountaineer's face and hazel eyes, he talked with a soft drawl. It was like slow syrup and his words always seemed to stick.

She sighed, sniffed, rattled a pot, put on her apron and began to fix breakfast. Finally, she came over and hugged me. She said, "I would have the luck to have a pesky boy for my only child. Happy birthday!" She was half-smiling. Not all the way. For some medical reason, she couldn't have any more children.

I knew not to put a shell in it inside the house, or even put it up to my shoulder. But I held it and rubbed it while my father watched, breaking the barrel and looking down that blue hole. I could almost hear it go *blam*.

I said to myself, *I christen thee Vulcan.* That was the Greek god of fire. I'd learned that in my last school in the States. It seemed right to give the gun a name.

Vulcan was the best gift I'd ever had. Thinking back, it was more than a gift. It was as if they were saying to me that I'd reached an age. At least my father was saying that. And I was more a man than any boy I knew. I was almost as tall as my mother and could throw a fifty-pound sack of meal across my shoulders and do fifty push-ups without getting breathy.

My father said, "There's somethin' else. C'mon outside." He seemed very pleased with himself. My mother followed us.

We had an enclosed back porch, a place to take off boots and heavy clothing in the winter, store skis, snowshoes and other things. Beyond that was our back yard, with a summer clothesline, a tin shed to smoke meat and fish, and a small vegetable garden to grow giant squash, turnips, beets, potatoes, beans and corn.

As I opened the back door and looked out, I saw a cardboard box with holes in it about the size of dimes. "Go open it up," said my father, grinning as if he'd pulled something over on us.

I flipped the lid back. Two small eyes looked up into the sky. They didn't really focus. They just sought light.

"It's a dog," I shouted.

My father didn't say anything.

I lifted him out. He was a small, brown woolly mound. His eyes hadn't been open too long. He began to squirm and make tiny noises. He was snub-nosed and still rat-tailed.

I heard my father laughing loudly and looked toward him. He said, "That's no dog, boy. You look again. Look close! He's about three weeks old."

I was sure he was a German shepherd pup. The nose was about the same; so were the ears. Yet there was something different about him.

My father whooped, "Boy, you got yourself a wolf pup!"

I couldn't believe it. I held him up, twisted and turned him; opened his mouth as if I could tell something that way. To me he still looked exactly like a shepherd.

My mother came over and looked at him, too. Then she turned to my father. "Jake Scofield, you've lost your mind," she said. But then she laughed, scratching along the pup's head. "Pretty thing, isn't he?"

I stuck a finger into his mouth, and he began to suck on it; then suddenly bit it. His teeth were sharp as tacks. Maybe he was a wolf.

"Nante found him yesterday, crawlin' out of a den," my father said. "Mother nowhere 'round. Couldn't leave him out there, could he?"

My mother arched her eyebrows.

Nante was the head Eskimo. He worked around the communications station out on Unigak and in the old cannery building, hunting and fishing on his days off.

"Nante said to call him Netsig," my father continued.

"What does that mean?" I asked.

My father shrugged. "Beats me."

"Well, we'll take care of him until he's able to do for himself," my mother said.

"I guess," my father agreed. "Meantime, boy, you got yourself a pet. Be sure'n thank Nante."

I said I would.

It was still hard to believe, a new .410 shotgun and a dog all in one day. A dog? Well, a wolf. But he looked and smelled and felt like a dog.

My mother sampled the air and suddenly ran for the back door. "Steaks are burnin'," she yelled, hurrying inside.

I put Netsig back in the cardboard box and went in for a breakfast of pan-fried deer steaks and hominy grits, something we usually reserved for Sunday mornings or holidays. Then my father caught the whaleboat down by the floating pier to go to duty.

[2]

We lived on the shores of Unigak Bay, pretty much wilderness. The bay is a shallow body of water on the Bering Sea, southwest of Norton Sound. To the north of us was Nome and Kotzebue, on either side of the Seward Peninsula; north of that was Wainwright and Point Barrow, and the Arctic Ocean. South was Nunivak Island, Kuskokwim Bay, Bristol Bay and the curving chain of the Aleutians, pointing like a dagger at Japan.

If you stood on our beach and stared straight out, you'd be looking at the Bering Sea, of which Unigak Bay was a small part. If you could look far enough out, you'd see St. Lawrence Island, with its villages of Gambell and Savoonga. Beyond that was Russia.

To the southwest, far out in the silent Bering was St. Matthew Island; below that, the lonely Pribilofs, home of the fur seals.

That's where we were, not too far below the Arctic Circle and toward the end of the earth. Sometimes, especially in winter, it seemed we were the only people alive.

It was not anything like Virginia, where we'd previously lived. In June, for instance, it is light all day and night. Just before midnight, there's a hint of dusky twilight for a few minutes. We'd sleep with the blinds drawn tightly.

Many people think there are snow, ice and darkness all year around along the Bering Sea. But we had a long summer, and the only snow we saw then was in patches on the mountain slopes. Even as far north as Icy Point, Wainright and Point Hope, there is good sunshine.

Sometimes the sky was so clear and greenish blue it didn't look real. In the spring and fall every star in the whole universe seemed to come and hang over Sedluk, very close to us.

My mother would say, "We have stars in our hats tonight, Dory." That's the way they looked, so close you could touch a point with a finger tip.

Long ago, when the Russians owned Alaska, Sedluk had been a fur-trapping outpost, and that's why our Russian church, with its yellow domes and spires sticking up from them, had been built. Then it had been a salmon fishery for a while. It was the farthest north salmon fishery in Alaska, way above the big runs of Bristol Bay.

But in 1933, we were told by Mrs. Thorkilsen, the oldest permanent resident, something had happened back in the mountains, maybe an earth movement, and Sedluk River changed course. The mouth filled up with silt, and only a brook coursed down it. The salmon couldn't swim up any more and chose another river miles south. The cannery closed down and was abandoned. The settlement became a ghost town.

Sedluk might simply have rotted away if the Navy hadn't decided in 1940 to put a radio listening station on Unigak Island, three miles offshore. The main purpose, my father said, was to monitor diplomatic and military messages from Japan.

The Navy had used the excuse that Russia had put an installation on one of their islands in the Bering Strait. Actually, the purpose of our highly classified station was to spy on the Japanese.

The Japanese did it to us, too. Sometimes we got very important information from those coded Japanese messages, my father said. They were relayed on to Washington and decoded there by some special machine.

My father, a radio expert, often took me out to Unigak, a great silent mound of grubby land and rock with radio towers sticking up from it like tall trees that had been stripped of branches. To the south end, there was a pinnacle rock, The Foot, maybe four hundred feet high. It was shaped like a foot, heel down to the ground. Unigak was sometimes a spooky-looking island, especially in the fog when just the radio towers were poking up as if they were floating.

Sedluk Settlement wasn't much of a town. It had two rows of wooden houses and a few other buildings along a single road that "came from nothing, and went nowhere," as my mother had written my grandpa and grandma Banner in Tennessee, when we first arrived in the summer of '40. It ran along the shore on a low ridge with the "sea houses" on the beach side of it, and the "inland houses," naturally, on the inland side. Back from it was a higher ridge, which was called Sedluk Ridge.

We lived on the inland side in a two-bedroom white frame house with our back porch facing Sedluk Ridge. There were fifteen new houses that the Navy had built on that side, and another fifteen on the beach side. At the north end was the new school, about a quarter mile from the settlement. There hadn't been any classes in it because the teacher the Navy had assigned hadn't made it to Sedluk.

At the far south end was the old cannery building, a long, low rambling shed that once had vats and equipment to can the salmon. Now the Navy used it for offices, storage and a small sick bay. It had a new steam plant for electricity, fired by fuel oil.

As for the other people in Sedluk, except for old Bakutan up on the high ridge in his sod hunt, which the Russians had called a *barabaras,* the small Eskimo population lived in the log ramshackles around the cannery. The only other person who lived in the ramshackles was Mrs. Thorkilsen, whose house was right opposite the cannery. She was tall enough to be a basketball player and had orange hair. She'd been the village nurse until her husband, the cannery boss, had died in the mid-thirties. He was buried out in her back yard. She knew more about the area than anyone and had the best singing voice in the village.

I'd heard that the Bering Coast Eskimo tribes were either Algemiut or Nushagagmiut, but I don't think the people at Sedluk were purebred from either tribe. In fact, they didn't seem to know or care what tribe they were from. But Nante, who had given me the wolf pup, insisted that he was pure Togiakmiut, from an ancient tribe around the Togiak River, on Bristol Bay.

Although the Eskimos trapped and hunted in the winter, and in summer fished, they all worked for the Navy now, except old Bakutan, who wouldn't work for anyone. They helped around the station and in the cannery building. I think they would have been happier just hunting and fishing, but the Navy paid a steady salary. Of course, they all went salmon fishing during the runs at a river some miles below us—the whole family going along to catch three or four thousand salmon.

Anyway, Sedluk had thirty-eight houses, the church, the school and the cannery building. Counting every soul, there were fifty-seven adults, including fourteen single sailors, mostly radiomen, five civilians, seven Eskimos; nineteen children of school age and six too young to go to school. There were forty-nine dogs and my wolf pup; five cats, none of which ever left the houses during the winter, and a pet raven owned by Mrs. Thorkilsen.

That's all there was to Sedluk, but I wouldn't have traded it for any other place in the world that summer of 1941 when I turned twelve.

[3]

After breakfast my mother said, "You build the pup a pen before you go off shooting that silly gun." She had a sour look on her face.

I didn't do it, just then. I put Netsig under one arm and the shotgun under the other and went four houses down the street to Char Midgett's.

During winter, in parka and pants, only her nose and mouth showing, it was hard to tell Charlotte Midgett from a boy. Sometimes I don't think she considered herself a girl, either. She could outrun

Max Unger and Tony DiSantis, and she could almost outrun me. We were the four oldest "Navy brats" in Sedluk. Char could also climb a cliff, paddle a kayak or shoot a fox.

Once, I made the mistake of getting into a scrap with her. I'd never been hit so hard by anyone. A looping right hand to my cheek, her knuckles in a stony fist. She could also belly punch, as Tony had learned.

But she was definitely a girl. Her hair was dark and soft, and the skin on her cheeks glowed. Her gold braces made her grin look crooked, but it wasn't. I suppose you could call Char pretty. I liked her because she never pulled for any favors.

"I wish I had him," said Char, cuddling the brown wool ball, rubbing him against her cheek. Char's father, also a chief radioman, had two spotted bird dogs and they were jumping up against her, trying to sniff the pup.

I showed her the shotgun, but she wasn't too much interested in it. Only Netsig.

We went over to Max's house, but he was still asleep. His mother wouldn't awaken him. She spoiled him. She said he'd been up late doing something. Max was a nature bug and collected things in bottles, shoe boxes, match boxes and tobacco tins. He was always sorting them. He read a lot and didn't talk much. He was big and chunky, with a square face and hair the color of wet sand. Max already knew he wanted to be a biologist or zoologist. Bookworm.

"Ask him to come over after he's had breakfast,"
I told his mother.

Then we got Tony out. He was small and wiry,
with a face like a dark ax, and seldom kept quiet.
He had a bad temper, and his brown eyes popped
like pinwheels when he got mad. He kept saying he
wanted to be a basketball player, but that was foolish
since he was so short. But he did rig a hoop in the
cannery building and shot baskets there.

The four of us got along all right and spent a lot
of time together. Sometimes we got tired of seeing
each other, but there was no one else our ages. Max
was thirteen, Tony and Char were both eleven.

Of the three of them, I was closest to Char. She
was always willing to do anything; go anywhere.
She could talk about a lot of things, sometimes pretty
crazy. She dreamed a lot and had a big imagination.

Tony was excited about the shotgun. He wanted
to take it out on the plain right away, but I had
to build the pen first. Netsig couldn't stay in that
cardboard box very long.

"Can you train a wolf like a dog?" Char asked, as
we crossed over to the cannery to get some spare
wooden boxes, chicken wire and nails.

I didn't know.

Tony said, "Sure you can." But he didn't know,
either, although he talked about it for five minutes.

Nante, who was a very handsome man of about
thirty, laughed at the idea of building a house for
Netsig but gave us the boxes, anyway. He did say some
people in Alaska and Canada had trained wolves.

"How did they do it?" I asked.

At that Nante grew serious. "Don't try it," he advised. "After he's big enough, maybe six or eight months, take him out on the plain and turn him loose."

I didn't say anything, but I already had other ideas. Somehow I knew that if I raised him from a pup I couldn't very well send him away. No one else but Char was thinking about that.

"That wouldn't be fair," she said to Nante.

Smiling at her, he tapped Netsig's snub nose. "This is a wolf. You'll find it out sooner or later."

We picked up a bottle and nipple from Chief Pharmacist Mate Robbins in the sick bay and then crossed to home again. Char fed Netsig some warm canned milk after Max arrived, and we all watched.

"How long will it be before you can wean him?" she asked.

"About five more weeks." At least, that's what my father had estimated at breakfast. Same as a dog.

He sucked at the nipple hungrily, just as any pup would. His eyes were half closed, his little tail stiff; every muscle in his small body was straining. Finally, I put him back in the cardboard box, and he went to sleep.

Then we began to build the shelter. We made the sides of the heavy chicken wire, put a floor in it, and a roof over it. Later, I knew it would be easy to tack wooden walls around it for protection against the cold.

You might know fat Max would say he didn't need

it. "Wolves are like huskies," Max said. "They can sleep out in the snow. They don't get cold because of their heavy coats. They stay warm at forty below."

I knew that, too. But most of the Eskimos had low log shelters for their dogs during the winter. Perhaps it was more than that. I was already beginning to think of Netsig as a dog, not a wolf.

We had lunch and then about two o'clock Char had to go home. Max and Tony had some chores to do so I went up on the plain alone. I took a dozen shells. I was anxious to try Vulcan now that Netsig was fixed up.

"You fire away from the ridge," my mother called out, standing in the back door frowning.

I said I would.

They didn't really worry about me too much when I hunted or fished alone. I'd been doing that for a long time, even back in Virginia when my father was stationed at the base in Norfolk. Crabbing with fish heads along the Elizabeth, shooting rabbits with a borrowed .22 back inland in the sages, or hopping those slow old Virginian coal jacks to get a ride for frog gigging in the feeder ditches that meandered in the marshes.

The plain extended four miles from Sedluk Ridge, sloping gently up to the mountain foothills. It was about seven miles wide, with the Sedluk River cut on the south end, and was covered mostly with tundra grass and wild flowers, which grew in great blankets during part of the summer.

Toward the north end were the pinnacle rocks.

They were like bumpy, upside-down ice cream cones or those castles you make with oozing sand. There were about fifty of them, all different heights. No one could explain how they got there.

The light was pink on the plain, I remember. Some days in summer it was amber. Then again it might be greenish. Light plays all kinds of tricks in the far north. Sometimes it was spooky. Twice, I'd seen an *ice blink*. It's like fifty million flash bulbs going off at once.

I went out about a mile and fired the .410. A couple of brant geese came by, too high to hit, but I shot at them anyway. Vulcan was a good gun, with only the slightest kick at my shoulder, and I let go with six shells.

Then I flopped down in the tawny tundra grass and stared up at the sky, enjoying the feeling of being alone. Except for the rustlings of the willow ptarmigan, a kind of arctic quail, it was dead quiet up there. Not anywhere on the whole plain was there a sign of any human.

I thought about the gun and Netsig, more sure than ever that I wanted to stay in Alaska as long as I lived, although my father wanted me to be a Navy officer. I hadn't told him, but lately, I was thinking of being a professional hunter or guide, combined with a bush pilot. I could see myself taking hunters out for bear or moose; landing a ski plane on a frozen lake.

Char and I sometimes made mind pictures. It was silly, I guess, but all sorts of things could make pictures in your head: *A poster at Traeger's trading post over at Unalakleet advertising Dory Scofield, Hunting and Fishing Guide; Dory Scofield and his wolf Netsig being interviewed by the Seattle newspapers.*

Finally, I decided to walk up to the pinnacle rocks. Sometimes there was small game around them. I'd seen wolverines up there several times. I wanted to fire Vulcan at a target.

It took about an hour to reach the rocks, and then I started winding in and out of them, the way you do trees that are laid out in a row. I came around the base of the third one and there was old Bakutan, his foot wedged by a big rock that had slid on loose, wet earth. He didn't say anything or ask for help. Just peered at me from those eyes of his that were like two holes drilled into brown granite. The pink light on his face was eerie.

I knew who he was, of course, but I'd never been this close to him. He never let people get too close. Most of the time, there was no expression on that broad, leathery face, worn by the sleet and wind off the Bering Sea. Those deep-hole eyes were cold as stream stones. I guess they frightened some people. And down wind, it was true you could smell him twenty feet away. Everyone in the settlement laughed and held their noses when he came down off the high ridge.

His wife had died about two months earlier, and old Bakutan didn't have another woman as yet. I'm not sure he liked or trusted anyone in the settlement except

Mrs. Thorkilsen. She fixed him a berry pie now and then. I know he hated the smaller children because they teased him.

I suppose he did look odd to some people, wearing that soiled hat of river otter; going around Sedluk in his summer skins instead of a cotton shirt, a dried bear's nose sewn to them for good luck.

I approached him cautiously and said, "Bakutan, I'll help you."

He just eyed me. He didn't even grunt. He was supposed to speak Yuk, a dialect of the old Yupik language of the Bering Coast tribes, but we'd heard he was really an Aleut. Someone said he had Russian blood in him, too.

I put Vulcan down and found a piece of wood, which somehow had come up from the beach. Standing on it, I used it for a lever to lift the rock while he pulled his foot out. The pain must have been bad, but he made no sound. Once, I looked into the deep-hole eyes. They held nothing.

He sat on the ground for a few minutes, rubbing his foot and ankle. Then he reached for his heavy rifle, and using it for support, got up. He began to hobble away, not looking back at me. I knew each step was painful.

"Do you want me to help you, Bakutan?" I called after him.

He didn't answer. I stood a moment, then grabbed Vulcan and ran after him. Still not saying anything, not even glancing at me, he leaned on my shoulder for three miles, hobbling toward his hut.

Because of his vicious sled dogs, I'd never gone near his *barabaras* before. But I'd seen it from a distance. Driftwood and whalebone were stacked around it. A couple of sleds stood end up against it. A single skylight of some kind of animal intestine was on the sod roof. The gut, stretched tight, served as a window pane. Nearby was his log food cache, up on stilts. Drying fish wobbled in the wind below it.

I got him to the outer door, but even then he didn't say anything. No thank you. He didn't even look at me. He went inside and closed the door, leaving me standing by the entranceway. Frightened of the chained dogs, snarling and snapping, I got away as fast as I could, thinking everyone was right about old Baku. He was a loony, ungrateful old man.

Over supper, before we had my birthday cake, I told my parents about it. My father just chuckled, but my mother said, "Don't go messin' around with that old man."

After supper, my father came out into the back yard where I was tallow polishing Vulcan's stock, over by Netsig's pen. He stood a moment, looking on and then sat down beside me. I'd drawn up a bench, the one my mother used for potting.

He kept looking at Vulcan, then finally said, "Your first gun, boy. That's somethin'."

While my mother always called me by my first name, up to that year I can never remember my father calling me anything but "boy." I didn't mind, but now and then I'd wonder why. I suppose it was just his mountain ways.

"You know," he went on, "guns an' men, real men, go together. Man's no good 'less he's got a gun, an' knows how to use it." Those hazel eyes lifted and searched my face.

I kept polishing.

Every once in a while, he'd talk to me about things like this, and I noticed it was never when my mother was around. He kind of shut her out, saying it was "gentlemun talk."

"This country was won on the end o' spittin' barrels, an' best you not forget it," he said.

"Yessir," I answered.

He lifted the gun from my hands and sighted it around. "More an' more, I been thinkin' about that naval prep school back in Maryland. Somehow, truly, I'm gonna get the money for you to go."

He'd talked about it before. It was a prep school for the naval academy exam. They helped you get into Annapolis. I didn't have the heart to tell him I'd been thinking, off and on, about being a hunting guide.

I said, "Yessir."

He grinned at me, put Vulcan back into my lap and stood up. "Not many sons of Navy chiefs have gone on to be officers, let alone admirals."

I nodded.

"Admiral D. B. Scofield, USN! Like guns an' men, that sure goes together, doesn't it? I hope I live to see that. Yessir."

He smiled down at me and went on back inside.

Whenever he talked about it, I could almost see

myself on the bridge wing of a carrier, dressed fancy and directing the task force, the planes climbing off into the sky from the flight deck. But then when I'd be alone I'd sometimes have those other thoughts.

Later, I put Vulcan on the table in my bedroom so I could see him shining. I left the light on. I brought Netsig in for a while to tumble him on my bed. It was hard to say when I went to sleep.

[4]

Toward the end of the next week, Baku came down off the ridge and approached our house carrying a caribou blanket. He gave it to my father, although I was standing right there. He said, "For him," meaning me, and then limped away.

I said, "Maybe he'll let me hunt with him now," and started to follow.

My father, staring after him, said, "No. Wait a day or so."

I couldn't understand that, and my father probably knew I was puzzled. He said, "Don't push him, boy. He's probably ready to make friends with you, but he'll be a sight more comfortable if you take it slow."

I nodded and went on around to the back yard. I got into the pen with Netsig and sat very quietly. For a few minutes he nosed around my legs and nipped at them. Then he drew away and put his head between his paws, staring at me until his eyes finally closed in sleep.

Already, there were signs that he wasn't a dog. He didn't whine like other pups do. Nor did he seem afraid when he was alone. And he was rougher than any pup I'd ever known.

I think it was four nights later when he heard his first wolf call. It came down from the foothills, clear and clean as struck steel on a cold dawn. Netsig froze, his head turned toward the mountains. Ears erect, nose up, he sniffed the air. I held him close and covered his ears.

I said, "Netsig, that's just an old wolf somewhere in the foothills. Don't pay any attention to him."

My father was sitting on the back step, as he often did on summer evenings, listening to the sounds from across the bay and the animal noises that came faintly across the plain.

He was puffing slowly on his briar, burley smoke wreathing around his head to keep the mosquitoes away. I knew he'd seen Netsig react to the howl, but it was a long time before he said anything.

Then: "Dory, he's a wild 'un. May not look it or act like it, but he's like ol' Baku. Part of the land. Long's he hears that call, he'll never be a dog."

I wanted him to stop talking but he went on, "I raised 'coons, crows, even a jumpy possum. You'd have a chance, maybe, if Netsig was crossed with a dog. But he's pure wolf."

"Mrs. Thorkilsen said to stay with him a lot, and that's what I'm doing."

There was another long silence, and then he said, "I didn't think it out, boy. You get yourself all attached to him, an' it comes to naught. You blame me, an' you'd be right. I shouldn't have let Nante give 'im to you."

Later, I let Netsig out of the pen. I rolled with him on the coarse grass and let him nip my hands and arms. But I went to bed that night hearing the wolf exercising his voice and seeing little Netsig stare off toward it. And he wasn't so little any more.

Next morning at five, I was off and up to the high ridge and old Bakutan's hut. I'd waited for a week to ask him if I could hunt with him; then I'd waited three more days to actually go up there and join him. He was gun hunting for a few weeks.

His dogs barked fiercely at me. They were on the heavy chains, but I stayed a respectful distance until he came out, carrying his 30.30 He grunted at me, which was about all I could ever expect out of him in the early morning.

"I got this gun for my birthday," I said, holding Vulcan up.

He glanced at it and started away.

We went south along the ridge toward the Sedluk River cut. He didn't speak and neither did I.

There were many stories about old Baku and some not very good. One story was that he'd fled the Aleutians because he'd killed a man. But that was fifty years ago or more. Mrs. Thorkilsen knew more about him than anyone. She said Baku was known to the Aleuts as "Tumgax-Siksinax," which meant "Breaker of Walrus Tusks." Even as old as he was, maybe seventy, he was very strong, and I soon found he could walk all morning without sitting down.

Most coastal Eskimos do not like to walk, but Baku didn't seem to mind. Although he was a marine Eskimo, he hunted and trapped inland, too. It was unusual, I heard. But then, Baku was always unusual.

We went along the river bank, working east. Then about eight-thirty, Vulcan tasted first blood: a wolverine. As almost anyone does, Baku hated them. They're vicious arch-backed weasels, not good for anything. They steal from food caches and break into huts. Not many animals are as mean as the wolverine.

We skinned the long-haired weasel. Wolverine fur doesn't ice up, so it makes a good liner for parka hoods. Then I put the pelt up high in an alder to pick up later.

We went on up river. Just being out there with him, I felt as though I were floating. No boy had ever hunted with him before, I was certain. I don't think many men had hunted with him in the last twenty years, when he got old and crotchety. So I watched everything he did.

In midmorning, Baku's 30.30 blasted out. He was about twenty yards to the side of me, moving silently on his sealskin boots. For a few seconds there was a thrashing in the brush, and then it was quiet.

I didn't even see the red fox, but Baku seldom missed anything, especially if it was a distance away. Up close, I'm sure he didn't see very well. As I walked along, I thought maybe this was the reason those stream-stone eyes said nothing when they peered out of the holes.

The fox's pelt was thin and sickly, not worth much, but we skinned him anyway and then headed for the plain. I soon learned that Baku liked to eat where it was warmest, in the direct sun.

Before long, he was sitting on a slab of rock in the tundra grass sucking on a piece of *muktuk,* which is whaleskin with about an inch of blubber on it, not saying anything, just looking out over the plain.

Later I discovered that he always brought *muktuk* along. It was the dessert that followed a meal of salmon or cod, and a few cold griddlecakes of oat and barley meal, a kind of Eskimo bannock that felt like rubber.

Packed in a square of cured walrus intestine and all squashed up sometimes, his meal never looked very good, but I suppose it tasted all right to him. I was just as glad to have my peanut butter and jelly sandwiches.

Appearances never seemed to bother Baku. Not much did. Not even the droning mosquitoes and noisy black flies that were circling our heads. He ignored them while I batted away.

I thought it might be a good time to talk about Netsig. "Nante gave me a wolf pup, and I want to train him as a dog."

He gave a hollow laugh, looked over at me, and shook his head. "No good for dog."

"Baku, I know that some people have trained them."

He nodded.

"Well, how did they do it?"

His old eyes roamed over the reaches for a while, then came back to me. "Stay with pup. Sit with him. Very quiet. Many hours." That's what Mrs. Thorkilsen had said, too.

Then the eyes went back to searching the plain, maybe looking for game.

"What else?"

He shook his head. I knew he wouldn't talk any more about it. He had that habit. He'd end a conversation and nothing could get him to talk. But maybe it was enough to start. Certainly, no one else around Sedluk knew as much about the land and animals as he did.

I don't know that it was true, but Mrs. Thorkilsen had said he could listen to the wolves talk to each other and understand what they were saying. She said Baku knew their hunting calls; their mourning howls. She said she'd seen him howl back at them. Their ears would come up and their eyes would flash.

Nante had told me that Baku could command a walrus to dive and then would know exactly when that walrus would surface and what he'd been eating. They stand on their heads to feed through their muzzles, sometimes at three hundred feet down.

They'd always drift south with the ice into the Bering Sea in autumn, and go back to the Arctic Ocean in the spring. Baku would let everyone know, to the very day, when the first walrus would appear.

He also knew about whales—the giant bottlenose, which fed off squid and octopus, and the humpback;

the beluga, the local white whale that could turn its head; the killer whale, which wasn't much of a killer at all.

A while back, he'd looked at one humpback and said, "Last year here."

Nante had asked, "Now, how do you know that, Bakutan?"

Baku had slapped his side and answered, "Scar!"

It made sense. The whale would scrape barnacles off his black hide and leave white scars. Baku would remember the scars and know the whale by them.

So whenever Baku talked about birds or fish or game or wolf pups, I listened.

[5]

The days of warm summer had begun to run, bounding along like fleet deer, and I spent most of the time with Baku or my father, seeing very little of Char Midgett; almost nothing of Tony and Max. By the third week in July 1941, we were beginning to stock food for the winter.

In our cold storage space beneath the back porch, dug into the ground beneath us that never really thawed more than a few feet down, we already had duck and willow ptarmigan, some of which I'd shot with Vulcan. We had two big swans for the holidays and caribou roasts, domestic deer steaks.

Although some food was brought in from Seattle, and some from Nome, most of the families in Sedluk lived off the land as the Eskimos had done for centuries. Except for sugar, coffee, bacon and things like that, we didn't really need too many store-bought supplies.

Unigak Bay and the rugged land around it was our store and butcher shop. The area was alive with game: brant and eider geese; humpbacked whitefish and sailfin graylings, Alaskan cod and salmon; beluga whales and seals and bear and caribou. All we needed was a gun or a trap or a fishing line. So it was important that we hunted and fished during the spring and summer. It wasn't just for the sport of it.

I suppose the most exciting thing that happened during midsummer was the announcement that our new teacher would arrive in late August.

Lieutenant McCall, the commanding officer at Unigak and the unofficial mayor of Sedluk, received the firm word in a dispatch from Seattle. Her name was Miss Sarah Etheridge.

I wasn't exactly overjoyed by the news. Neither was Tony DiSantis. But Char and Max Unger were pleased.

Our one-room wooden school had been completed in the summer of '40. The Navy had promised a teacher that year, but winter set in before she could arrive. Now the Navy was making good its promise.

I would just as soon have kept up with the correspondence courses we'd had the last winter, leaving me more time to ice fish and work on carving bone or building model airplanes. Tony felt the same way for other reasons. He was making scrapbooks on basketball players.

By the time the courses got to Chicago, where they were graded, and then back to Sedluk, it had been early spring. What the arrival of Miss Etheridge really meant was that we'd all have to go to school six or seven hours a day instead of the three we'd spent on mail school.

Aside from the parents, I think Char was looking forward to the new teacher's arrival more than anyone else. She came running over, yelling, "Have you heard about it? Have you heard about it?"

I said I had, and so what.

"I hope she's young and pretty," Char said.

"What difference does it make?" I asked.

"Aren't you excited?"

"Nope."

I was cultivating along the corn rows in our garden. I had to do it every two weeks.

"Lieutenant McCall said she's been teaching in a city school in San Francisco. She graduated from Colorado State, and she's highly recommended."

"That's nice," I said, and went on hoeing.

"You mean you'd rather study out of those dull correspondence books than have a teacher this winter?"

I nodded.

Char got angry. "Well, you can stay stupid if you want to but not me."

I laughed and asked who had recommended Miss Etheridge so highly.

"The Navy did."

"What does the Navy know about teachers?" I asked.

Char's face was storming up, some red showing under her cheekbones. We argued another ten minutes, and then she whirled around and took off across the back yards, fuming. It was never too hard to get Char to the boiling point.

I told Tony about it, and for the next two weeks anytime we'd see Char we'd get a crack in at Miss Etheridge. Finally, for a week she wouldn't talk to us.

It wasn't that I had anything against the new teacher. I just didn't like the idea of being cooped up in that school week after week. And, somehow, my luck seemed to change after the big announcement from Lieutenant McCall. It turned bad.

A few days later I decided to take Netsig out on the plain and headed northwest toward the pinnacles. He was almost four months old now and weighed about thirty-five pounds. He wasn't too young to begin learning, even if it was only to come and go on call. I also had in the back of my mind the idea of training him for hunting. My father said it was foolish, and Baku agreed, but I thought there was no harm in trying.

Except for the color of his coat, he looked like a young German shepherd now. He was losing his puppy hair and turning a grizzly gray. His coat was thickening up. His tail was getting bushy, and he was beginning to lose his milk teeth. He was still clumsy on those big paws but that was the only puppy trait I could notice.

We moved across the plain toward the rocks where I'd found Baku wedged in and Netsig flushed some quail, same as any hound. He couldn't catch them, but his legs went flat out trying. I watched, laughing as Netsig put on the brakes to tumble head over tail.

The light had turned from yellowish green to almost pure yellow and the air was crisp. Trudging on, I practiced howling now and then, causing Netsig, criss-crossing ahead, to sniff the air and circle back. When he realized it was only me, he'd grin and romp away.

Some people said it was nonsense that wolves talked to each other, but even before I knew Baku I believed they did. I'd often lie in bed and listen to them out on the plain. Owls and whippoorwills didn't really talk to each other, but wolves did.

Walking on, I wondered if someday I could get Baku to teach me how to talk to Netsig. I was sure Baku could call a pack in, deep toning and wailing, any time he wanted.

"Close your eyes, Dory, and Bakutan can make you shiver with his howling," Mrs. Thorkilsen had said.

Yet I knew that none of this made sense. Why should I be thinking about howling if I wanted Netsig to be a dog? Sometimes my thoughts wrecked up on each other. What I wanted, I guess, was for Netsig to stay a wolf but act like a dog.

Midmorning I got up to the pinnacle rocks and lost Netsig for a few minutes. I called him and then howled, but there was no sign of him. It was not really a worry because I knew he was just snooping around somewhere, sampling the ground near the rocks.

Finally, I found him inside a shallow cave, under a rock overhang. He was tensed up and sniffing.

I asked, "What are you doing in there, you ol' pup?"

Netsig paid no attention. So I got down on my hands and knees, sticking my head inside. I saw hair and droppings and knew immediately that a mother wolf had raised a litter in the cave, maybe last spring. Maybe this was where Nante had found him.

The opening wasn't much more than a foot and a half high, so the grown wolves would have had to crawl in. With a sinking feeling I watched him and wondered what was going through his head. I could see his eyes in the dim crack of light from the den entrance. They were bright and there was a strange glint in them.

Hoping to snap him out of it I said, "Netsig, you're a dog now. Not a wolf any more. Come out of there."

The pup was busy with his own thoughts and kept snuffling around until I reached in and jerked him out. He squirmed to get away so I carried him at least a quarter mile from the den before I put him down.

But less than half an hour later, I lost him again. This time we were nearing the end of the pinnacle row, and Netsig disappeared behind them, about a hundred yards ahead of me.

Suddenly, there was a chilling noise that sounded like broken glass being scraped across tin. It was a snarl, ugly and menacing. Then I heard a low howl, like the sound Baku had said was a wolf's hunting howl. *It had to be Netsig.*

I ran toward the sounds, flipping the safety off Vulcan. I pulled up in time to see Netsig poised; stiff except for the tip of his tail. It lashed slowly back and forth, as if he hadn't made up his mind what to do.

The wolverine, dark brown with a bushy tail and a chestnut streak up his sides, had his beady eyes fixed on Netsig. His teeth were bared and his weasel back was arched like a pulled bow. The wolverine was up against a big pinnacle, trapped on both sides. No place to go except up the rocks.

But wolverines never ran, I knew. They always fought. At twenty snarling pounds, they could kill a cougar or send a bear loping on his way. I was sure Netsig didn't know what he was facing. But all morning, he'd flushed those quail and lost them. Now he had something in front of him that wouldn't run or flutter.

I raised Vulcan, sighted and fired but saw a blur of gray moving, too. Not a second after I'd hit the wolverine and wounded him, Netsig sunk his teeth into the weasel's back. The two animals exploded in the yellow air with sounds so terrible that they haunted me for weeks.

Trapped and dying, the wolverine locked onto Netsig's leg. As I ran closer, they twisted and turned, teeth tearing flesh; screams shattering the quiet of the plain. Then it was all over—Netsig on his side on the ground, eyes bulging; breath coming in harsh gasps.

The dead wolverine's jaws were still clamped on Netsig's leg. Almost sick seeing what he'd done to the pup's left hind leg, I pried that ugly mouth open with my gun barrel.

The leg was ripped and torn, almost shredded; bleeding hard. I kicked the wolverine away, cursing him, and pulled my shirt off. I wrapped Netsig's leg in it, telling the shuddering pup that everything would be all right.

Then, leaving the gun by the pinnacles, knowing I could get it later, I started home, cradling Netsig in my arms, running a ways and then walking; then running again.

[6]

My mother was in the kitchen. She took one look at the bloody shirt wrapped around Netsig's leg and hurried to the phone to call my father on Unigak.

While I rubbed Netsig's head, repeating over and over, "Easy, boy, easy," I heard my mother mention Pharmacist Mate Robbins who usually took care of all emergencies at Sedluk. But my father suggested Mrs. Thorkilsen. She knew more about treating animals.

"He'll be home as quick as he can get a boat over," my mother said.

We took Netsig down to Mrs. Thorkilsen's and she spread a sheet on the kitchen table. I lifted him up

there, stroking along his side and belly to calm him.
He was quieter now; his breathing had slowed. But
his weak moaning was a horrible sound.

After she unwound the shirt from the leg, Mrs.
Thorkilsen said, "It's not good."

I couldn't bear to look at it.

Mrs. Thorkilsen took her medicine kit from a cup-
board, asking mechanically, "What got him?"

"Wolverine," I answered.

She shook her dyed orange hair. "Those are the
worst animals that ever lived. You should know better,
Dory, than to let him get near a wolverine. Only thing
that can beat 'em is a porcupine. Even then, the wolverine don't die until the porcupine quills poke holes
in his stomach. Porcupine's long dead."

She was looking down at me, big nose pointed at
my forehead. She looked down on almost everyone. She
was a head and a half taller than my mother. She
had green eyes and with that flaming orange hair she
was something to see. Her hands were the size of
baseball mitts and always red.

"He didn't know what it was," I said. "Please help
him."

Mrs. Thorkilsen sighed. "I'll do what I can." She
went into the front room for a lamp so she'd have more
light. When she got back, she said, "I've treated cats,
dogs, and reindeer but never a wolf. I don't even
know how much of a dose to give him. Dog dose,
maybe. You better hold his jaws."

I held them tight, telling Netsig it wouldn't hurt

much. He gave a little start when the needle went into his flank. Soon, his eyes were dazed.

My father arrived, took a long look at the leg and listened to Mrs. Thorkilsen say, "Some of this muscle is gone. There's a tendon snapped here. I can't repair that, Chief. Maybe a vet could. I doubt it. He'll just hobble as long as he lives."

I was kneeling by the kitchen table, holding Netsig. My father looked down at me. He said quietly and firmly, "Boy, you'd be doin' him a favor if you'd let me take him out on the prairie."

I knew exactly what he meant. In Virginia, we had Duke, a big red Chesapeake. A garbage truck hit him one morning, breaking his back. My father had put him out of pain.

I couldn't speak. Everything was caught in my throat.

"He'll hobble the rest of his life! If we have to turn him loose someday, he'll not last a night out there. Even the wolves, his own kind, may kill him."

I didn't answer.

"I'm talkin' about a crippled animal, boy," my father said with some heat in his voice.

I put my head down on Netsig's warm, thick coat. I could hear his breathing and feel it. It was slow and steady. He was alive. He'd be all right. Then everything inside me seemed to be flooding out, and I couldn't speak to my father. I knew he was looking down at me.

I heard Mrs. Thorkilsen say, "Well, I'll try."

"Jake, least we can do is try. For Dory's sake," my mother said.

Funny, she'd never really liked Netsig, but now she was protecting him.

There was a silence for a moment, and then my father said, "It's not the right thing to do, Cece, but let's see about it."

I stayed hunched over Netsig until they finished. His coat was wet where my face had been against it. Every once in a while, he'd stiffen when they'd do something painful to his leg. But he never made a sound.

My father said admiringly, "That'd been a dog, would of taken three men to hold him down."

I carried Netsig home and stayed with him in the pen for a long time, talking softly to him, rubbing his head and back. As the drug wore off, he made moaning sounds. He was so weak he couldn't lift his tail.

Sitting beside him, stroking his back, I felt very guilty. I knew I should have waited until he was older to take him beyond the ridge lines. More than that, I should never have tried to hunt with him. Perhaps that was what Baku had really been trying to tell me. I'd turned him into a pet, not a fighter.

After Netsig went into a deep sleep I made certain nothing could get at him in the pen and then went back into the pinnacles to get Vulcan. I did a silly thing. I shot that wolverine again even though he'd been dead for hours.

At supper that night, my father didn't say much about Netsig, just asked how he was. Later, I went out to the front room. He was reading the *National*

Geographic. He liked to read about far-off places or fights between armadas.

I told him it had been my fault, not Netsig's.

He put the magazine down and nodded. "Yep, that's true."

To make up for it, I told him I was going to take extra care of Netsig and nurse that leg back to normal.

He nodded again. "I hope so."

As I was leaving the room, he called out in afterthought, "Something you ought to clearly understand, boy."

I stood in the doorway.

"That leg'll never be the same. You've got a gimpy dog now, and you best realize it. You may have to fight battles for him worse'n today. Much worse. This same kind of thing has happened to other boys before when they thought they knew more than they did."

"Yessir," I said, but I did notice he called him a dog instead of a wolf.

"Burden's on you," he said, picking up the magazine again.

I went on out to the pen, thinking about it.

In the next week I began to know what he meant. Even that next morning, I knew. Netsig was standing up in the pen when I came out. Wagging his tail, he hopped across on three feet, holding his left hind leg up. He was grinning.

He wasn't blaming anybody and that was part of the burden.

[7]

One morning in late August I went up to Baku's and shouted for him. About five minutes later, he came out.

As I always did, I said, "Good morning, Bakutan."

He belched loudly from his breakfast, as he usually did, squinted at me and looked off at the weather.

Sedluk was wrapped in fog, and even Unigak Island was hidden by a low mist, only the tall radio towers sticking up from it. But there was brown early light on the plain. It would clear up later.

As we walked southeast toward the river, I said, "Baku, I will have to start school soon. But I can hunt with you in late afternoon until we lose light."

He wouldn't be hunting much past the first of October, anyway. He'd ice fish some and run trap lines for fox, beaver, mink and land otter, but he'd probably sleep a lot during the winter inside the dark sod house. He didn't answer me.

I said, "Our teacher will be here in two or three days, and I'll have to go to school until early afternoon. I don't want to, but I have to. Do you understand?"

His eyes swung around to me. "Tobacco?" he asked.

I grinned at him. "Yes, I'll keep bringing tobacco."

Baku grunted. I guess it was approval.

I didn't want to admit it to myself, but I'm sure one big reason why he let me go with him was because I gave him tobacco. He didn't smoke but traded it off for something he might want.

My father had wondered since late June why the burley mix in the glass humidor in the front room kept going down. Once he did ask me if I'd started to smoke. I hadn't and told him that. He'd walked out of the room, looking very puzzled. My mother didn't smoke, of course.

For a while, after I'd brought Baku his first small sack of tobacco, he'd name off the birds and animals with a gesture or word. Puffins and terns out on Unigak; black-footed albatross; on shore, the kittiwakes and murrelets and water pipits. The way he'd pronounce them I'd often have to look them up in the encyclopedia.

He'd also show me the different seals, often giving me the Eskimo names. The bearded seal, for instance, is an *oogruk*. Or he pronounced it that way.

I walked beside him over the plain grass, carrying Vulcan, now and then flushing up a ptarmigan but not shooting at it.

Far away, a lone duck crossed the sky. Baku nodded toward it and muttered, *"Oh-kingu-luk."* A squaw duck.

It was a sign that winter was approaching because the tough-meated sawbills were the only ones around after November. The great clouds of eiders that darkened the sky in late May were already gone.

We walked on.

Back from the river banks, the whole valley was still pretty green. The cold water from the mountain runs, clear as glass, made the valley burst into color

in the spring after the snow melted. There were small
stands of alders and stubby birch along it. Some wil-
lows. Farther on up, there were some stands of spruce.

At the point that the river used to pour through the
treeless foothills, before the earth movement changed
its course, there were blueberry bushes and fireweed
and a plant my father said was a devil's club.

There weren't many places in the world as pretty
as this little valley, and aside from Baku and myself,
I'd bet not more than fifty people a year went up it.
So it was, I thought, *our* valley, set like an oasis in the
harsh land.

There was plenty of game feeding along the river,
but they'd break and run as we worked eastward.
Up on the ridges we saw caribou fleeting ahead but
paid them no mind.

In the spring and early summer, it would be different. Then Baku would be fishing and hunting for
food. Baku usually shot and fished only for what he
needed. He did not needlessly kill. Good hunters never
did, nor good fishermen. My father had drummed that
into me since I was five.

And while he never left his *barabaras* without the
30.30, I felt almost certain Baku would rather be hunting again with a bow and arrow, a snare or a spear.
The one time I'd peeked inside his hut, I'd seen two
bows and several sharp, shining spears in the dim yellow
light of his blubber lamp.

Once, when the 30.30 crashed out, echoing for miles,
he'd grunted, "Arrow better." But he was too old to
hunt with a bow and arrow.

I kept thinking I would have liked to live back in the days when no one but the Eskimos and Indians were around Unigak Bay; when they didn't use rifles, and have outboard motors on their umiaks, the big skin boats.

Sometimes when we went back through the valley or over the plain, I could imagine how it was when there were great herds of caribou, instead of the small ones we saw now; when the sea otters still numbered in the hundreds of thousands, and when the fox, not knowing what man was, would come three feet from him and bark.

Still, I admit I got a thrill when I pressed the trigger of the .410 and knew it was on target. That was natural, my father said. It was all right as long as I stuck to Baku's law and shot only what we needed. But Baku's law was often strange and confusing.

After eating up on the plain in early afternoon, sprawled out in the lichen in the warm sun, we went back down into the valley, moving along the south bank until we got to the stand of spruce about three and a half miles inland, where the land starts rising sharply to the rugged mountains. There were clumps of wild berry bushes near the spruce, and game could usually be found there in late afternoon.

We were going through the brush near the spruce and all I could see of Baku, twenty yards away, was that bobbing river otter hat. But I knew we were getting near the dead-end ravine and lifted the safety catch on Vulcan. Sometimes, we'd see some wolverines there.

I rounded the low bushes at the mouth of the ravine and stopped dead still, my feet lumps of ice and my mouth wide enough to swallow a doughnut whole.

Not a hundred feet away was a brown bear having himself a feast, his big mouth tearing away at the blueberries, shaking the bushes.

The sound of the river had covered our footsteps, and he'd been so busy stuffing himself he hadn't sniffed us. His big head swung around, and he looked at me, eyes like widening circles in a still pool, growing larger each second.

I don't know how long we stood there like that, but then out of fright and surprise, I fired, hitting him in the chest and mouth. He let out a cough; the tiny .410 pellets didn't do much more than sting him hard.

I saw how big he was now. Maybe a thousand pounds. He coughed again, making a sound like metal snapping, and looked over his shoulder back into the ravine. There was no way out. The only way was right down my throat.

Then he began bounding toward me, a half ton of brown shag with jaws wider than Baku's heavy traps and just as strong.

I dropped the gun and ran for the river, him crashing along behind me like a mad, loose steam roller, rumbling sounds coming out of his belly.

I saw Baku standing by the edge of the river, watching us split the low brush. I yelled at the old loon, wondering why he didn't shoot. He had his gun up.

I ran past him, splashed the few feet across the river and swung up into the first spruce, so frightened I could hardly breathe. Then I looked around.

The bear had stopped about fifty feet away from the old man and stood there staring at him, making low rumbling noises like lions do in front of a trainer.

Baku was sighting on him all right, but was standing motionless, a small, compact statue, feet planted wide apart, body leaning a little toward the bear. I wondered why he didn't shoot, yet I knew better than to shout at him. You never shout at a man holding a loaded gun.

They stayed that way for almost a minute, the bear's head turning angrily from side to side, jaws half-open and berry spittle still dripping out.

Then he looked over Baku's head and up to me half-hidden in the spruce. He let out another low growl, sniffed the air, and suddenly ambled off into the brush, toward the mountains, still making those angry noises.

Baku lowered his gun.

He'd actually stared that bear down. You could hear his noises growing fainter as he went away.

I took some deep breaths, my heart pounding so hard I could hear it in my ears.

Without looking back at me, the old man disappeared into the ravine. I shouted after him, but he didn't answer.

In a moment, he came out carrying Vulcan. I was down out of the tree by then and wanted to talk to him about the bear. I couldn't figure out why he hadn't shot him. Even though he didn't see well close-up, he couldn't have missed that big body.

Baku didn't even glance at me. First rock he came to, he took the .410 by the barrel and broke the stock. It splintered good, and I knew it was rendered useless.

For a moment, I couldn't find words to say. He *was* crazy.

He flung it at me, the broken stock hanging, and turned on his heels, walking back down river. I shouted after him, "Why'd you do that?"

He didn't answer, just kept moving ahead, silent as a cat on those seal boots, not making a rustle or even cracking a twig.

I walked about fifty feet behind him, carrying the barrel and busted stock, keeping my mouth closed and making myself stay angry so no tears would come. It was hard to believe what that old loon had done.

We crossed the plain that way, and Baku never once looked back. He knew I was right behind him. He also knew, I think, that I was so mad I could have banked that barrel right off his otter hat.

When we got to his hut, I ran the last few steps to catch up and then yelled at him, "Why'd you break my gun?"

Bakutan turned slowly and stared at me. He said, "You go shoot tundra hare, wolverine. Not bear."

I raged at him, "I'll shoot anything I want."

"You shoot bear with small gun, kill us both," he said gutturally, disgust hanging on each word.

I didn't know what to say.

"Go house," Baku ordered. "Leave gun."

He wrenched it out of my hands.

When things go bad, they often go all the way. Struggling with him, I slipped in the mud and slid downhill to within two feet of his dogs. They lunged at me, barking and snarling. I was so close I could smell their hot, foul breath.

Baku drove them off with a piece of driftwood, giving them some brutal blows. Then he jerked me to my feet.

"Go house," he said, as if I was five years old.

Mud-stained and with mud in my mouth, I went on down the ridge until he couldn't see me. Then I sat down and cried.

I hadn't cried in two years, except about Netsig.

During supper, I told my father that I'd left Vulcan at Baku's so he could make a new stock. I was too ashamed to tell him what had really happened. Instead I said I'd stumbled and busted the stock. He frowned but didn't say anything. I didn't tell him about the bear.

My mother sighed. "I just wish you wouldn't go off with that old man. Something bad's going to happen some day." She'd been saying that since June so it wasn't anything new.

I took Netsig to bed with me that night, but he was restless and kept sniffing the caribou blanket, which smelled of wild animal. He stiffened once when he heard a wolf howl. But then he nestled close to me and went to sleep.

I went to sleep, too, after a while, thinking about Baku. He was a terrible old man.

[8]

The USS *Beaufort Sea* came in during the night. An old storeship with a high stack that usually coiled out thick smoke, she anchored west of Unigak. Big ships could not come close to shore in most places in western Alaska. Cargo was barged in.

While I was having breakfast, I could hear the noises and shouts down at the floating dock as stores were unloaded. It would be our last ship until April or May. Whaleboats and our heavier powered utility boat tugged the small barges back and forth. All the enlisted men were turned-to to push laden hand trucks to the cannery.

The *Beaufort Sea*, a Hog Island type that had served in World War I, had sailed up from Seattle, and for a few weeks we'd have all the fresh fruit we could eat, even bananas. That was always a treat.

Tony banged on our back door. "Let's take the rowboat out to the *B-Sea*," he shouted in. I said okay and he went off to get Max and Char. My mother was down in the cannery helping with inventory.

We'd talked about it earlier. We weren't supposed to use the rowboat, but everyone was always so busy when stores were being unloaded that we thought we wouldn't be noticed. In the past, every time the *B-Sea* (which was what North Pacific sailors called her) had come in, we'd been booted off the utility boat. Lieutenant McCall thought we might get hurt when the cargo booms swung around to drop slings of boxes and crates on the barges. He was a worry wart, anyway.

I met them down on the dock about ten minutes later. Max was a little reluctant to go, but Tony egged him on. Char was hot to go. None of us had ever seen the *B-Sea* close-up. Also, once we got out there we knew the sailors would toss us candy and ice cream from the ship's exchange.

We stood around for a little while, watching the boxes come in, all labeled "USN CommSta-Unigak, Sedluk, Alaska," and soon the sailors forgot we were even there. Then Tony nodded and we went to the rowboat, which was tied up on the north side of the dock. Nonchalantly, we got in. Tony and I manned the oars, pulling away.

One sailor yelled, "Where you kids goin'?"

"Just up the beach," Tony shouted back; then muttered, "Keep rowin'."

A few minutes later we changed course toward Unigak, figuring to skirt North Point and then come down on the *B-Sea* on the other side of the island. There was no wind, and the surface of the strait was like a starched bed sheet.

Max had settled down now and wasn't so nervous. Char, sitting in the stern with him, was jabbering about a sewing machine that was supposed to be on the *B-Sea* for her mother. They'd ordered some patterns from Monkey Ward's in Chicago.

Tony, between pulls, said, "Hey, I bet that was the box I saw comin' off one barge, all stoved in."

Char scooped up some water in her palm, flipping it into his face. Tony took a short stroke on his oar, spattering both Char and Max. I yelled for them to knock it off, and Max said we could put him ashore if we wanted to have a water fight out there. The sea was cold.

By nine-thirty, we were off North Point, beginning to round it, angling out to the ship, which was in deeper water three miles or so off, when her whistle sounded five or six times. Then the whistle at Sedluk answered.

Char said, "Look!"

We looked west, and saw a high wall of fog moving swiftly in. That's why the *B-Sea* had signaled, telling the boats to secure until the fog had passed.

Max said, "Oh, boy."

Although the fog was sometimes so thick you couldn't see a light twenty feet away, there was nothing to be worried about. I told Tony, "Let's head for North Point."

The bank was moving fast, but it looked as if we could get almost to the island before it caught us.

The oarlocks knocked away steadily, and there wasn't much said as we raced for North Point, but in about five minutes I knew we weren't going to make it. Then suddenly the fog swept over us, and Unigak disappeared in a wet, gray roll.

"Now, we're in trouble," Max said. "You and your free candy and ice cream."

"Shut up, Max," Tony said.

Max hunched down glumly in the stern. He looked like an old man with mumps.

We rowed on. It was a very wet fog, and we began to get cold. None of us were dressed for it. After about ten minutes, I thought we should stop and listen. If we were still headed for North Point, we should be able to hear the light splash of the water against the rocks. So we drifted a moment, dead quiet.

Tony and I looked at each other. There was no sound. We were thinking the same thing—we'd missed the point.

Max piped up. "How fast does this thing travel?"

"On this water, three or four miles an hour," I said. It was just a guess.

"Which way was the tide setting when the fog rolled in?" Max asked. That was Max, the brain.

Tony and I looked at each other again. Char was staring off into the soup but knew what was going on. "West," I said. "Out!"

Max wiped his nose. "You've missed North Point."

It would have been great to kick Max over the stern.

"We can drift a thousand miles now," he said.

Char spoke up. "When the tide changes, we'll just drift back to Sedluk." However, I noticed she was shivering.

"You hope," Max said, hunching down some more and buttoning his shirt collar. We were wearing sweaters and they had beads of water all over them. Our pants were getting wet.

Tony said, "Let's row some more."

I told him that didn't make sense because we were probably headed in the wrong direction. "Let's just sit and listen."

Tony got angry. "And float all the way to Russia?"

"If you've got eyes to see through the fog, go ahead and row," Char snapped at him.

All of a sudden everybody was mad at everybody else. Tony started pulling on his oar, but we just went in circles. He finally stopped, and we drifted over the satin smooth water, trapped in the murk. The only sound was the occasional flop of a fish.

Max mumbled once, "We might ground on St. Lawrence Island." St. Lawrence was a good two or three hundred miles from Sedluk.

"Be quiet," Char said.

It was getting pretty miserable out there. Our noses were dripping, and we tucked our hands under our belts to keep them warm.

About noon, we heard music in the distance. The sound was faint, but it was definitely music. It had to be Sedluk. Tony said, "Let's go." So we started rowing again toward the music, pausing now and then to keep our bearing. It was a radio, playing loud, and I made a guess that it was out of the cannery.

About ten minutes later, we could hear voices now and then mixed in with the music. We were homing in on Glenn Miller's "Sunrise Serenade." I figured we could tie the boat up, and nobody would ever know we'd been gone.

But then a shape loomed out of the fog, and it

wasn't the floating dock. Forty more feet, and we bumped up against the riveted, rusting side of the USS *Beaufort Sea*. A few yards away, we could see her heavy anchor chain angling down into the water. We could hear her pumps and machinery working inside the hull. We could smell the *B-Sea* too. At noon, there is always a good food smell around ships.

I yelled, "Hello, up there."

In a moment, we could see a vague face peering at us from above. On top of it was a khaki chief's hat. "What are you doin' down there?" he asked.

"We got lost," Tony shouted.

He grunted, then yelled back, "Work along the hull 'til you get midships. There's a gangway down." We heard other voices and some laughter from the deck.

He grunted, then yelled back, "Work along the hull until we saw the extended sea gangway. Several of the Unigak whaleboats were tied to it. Aft of that were two small barges, half loaded. A forlorn cargo boom stuck out over the side.

Several men stood on the upper gangway platform, looking down. One was an officer, an ensign. He said, "Tie it up and come on aboard."

By that time, the captain of the *B-Sea* had come out. His name was Wrightson. I'd seen him ashore in Sedluk before. He said, "You kids were lucky. If you'd missed us, you could have drifted all the way to Yokohama."

Max, getting out of the boat, turned toward us and nodded. Char got out as Tony was lashing the line to a gangway stanchion. Then we all started up.

Lieutenant McCall had joined Commander Wrightson. He'd been having coffee aboard when the fog
came in and stranded him.

Wrightson asked, "You know these kids?"

The lieutenant nodded bleakly. "The fearless four-
some. No, I take that back. The Unger boy's all
right. He's got some sense."

Max smiled widely at the lieutenant, but we all
looked at him as if he were a rotten fish. We were
huddled together on the quarter-deck.

Commander Wrightson said to the ensign, who was
the watch officer, "Take 'em below, get 'em warm,
and feed 'em." We followed the ensign, none of us
looking back.

He took us to the fiddley, which is a grating in the
engine room above the boilers. It was like a low oven
in there. We stayed about twenty minutes, warming
up, putting our sweaters over the pipe railing to dry.
Then we went down to the enlisted men's mess and
had lunch. We also had ice cream and candy, so it all
worked out fine.

The fog lifted about four o'clock, and we went back
to Sedluk with Lieutenant McCall, the rowboat towing behind. On the floating dock, the lieutenant said,
"Any of you touch that boat again, and I'll have you
confined to quarters for a week." He wasn't too happy.

Part II

THE TEACHER

[1]

My mother claims it was August 28, '41 when Miss Etheridge arrived, but I think it was the thirtieth. I know I stayed away from old Bakutan's hut for three days.

Whatever, almost everyone in Sedluk except Baku was on the shore at two o'clock in the afternoon, staring up at the slate-colored sky and listening for the distant roar of engines.

There was a long sign, red letters on white oilcloth, that said, "Welcome, Miss Etheridge!" It was draped over the back end of the cannery so it would be the first thing she saw when she got out of the seaplane from Dutch Harbor, the U. S. Navy base out on the Aleutians. She'd been flown there from Seattle.

Four of the enlisted men from the station on Unigak were standing out on the floating dock as an honor guard. They wore dress blues with white canvas leggings and stood at parade rest, butts of their rifles by their gleaming shoes.

Soon, the seaplane, a big, blue two-engined aircraft

with floats on its wings, broke out of the cloud cover and skimmed in low over Unigak Strait, while the pilot searched the water for anything that might rip his hull. They always did this, even the tiny fur trader or sportsmen float planes that would visit us during the summer.

The water was as smooth as thick pork gravy and almost the same color. It was free of driftwood, as it usually was in August, so the pilot circled out around Unigak Island and came in for his approach, finally landing in the strait like a great blue swan, the propellers beating up white spray, the thunder of his engines echoing off the ridge behind us.

A whaleboat was out there waiting for him. We watched as they took the mailbags out of the seaplane hatch. Usually, this was the big occasion around Sedluk, one we looked forward to every week. But not today.

Then we saw the sailors help a figure into the boat. It was Miss Etheridge, of course, and everyone cheered and clapped. I joined in but not very enthusiastically.

I was standing on the pontoon dock with Char, Tony and Max, not far from the honor guard. "She looks no bigger than a toothpick," I said, hoping to get a rise out of Char.

It worked. Char said angrily, "You can't tell anything from here."

We couldn't, of course. We could barely see her in the whaleboat which was pounding toward shore, the exhaust making a smoky blue fuss.

Tony laughed. "I can tell she's fifty and has false teeth."

Char gave him a furious look. He was lucky she was holding flowers. In the morning, Char and Max had gone up to the plain to pick the few wild flowers that were still left. Char had on a dress, first time I'd seen her in one since the Christmas Day party of '40. But I guess she wanted to be sure Miss Etheridge made no mistake about her sex.

When the boat was about two hundred yards away, Lieutenant McCall shouted, "Now, everybody remember, let's try to make this an official welcome."

He was talking about the honor guard and the speech he planned to make. He had a bald head and a white, bony face, but still looked like an admiral instead of a lieutenant in his gold-buttoned bridge coat and white scarf. It was almost too warm for the coat but he had it on anyway. His hat covered his baldness.

When the boat came alongside, we got our first good look at Miss Etheridge. She wasn't fifty years old as Tony had predicted, but she was every bit of thirty. Although she was bundled up in a fur coat, as if it was freezing weather in Sedluk instead of summer, you could tell she was a toothpick. She wore a fur hat and what appeared to be rain galoshes.

Tony started to laugh softly, and I joined him. If no one else had been around, Char might have pushed us off the dock. Her eyes were blazing.

Lieutenant McCall began to clap again and the applause went all along the dock. Then the people on shore began to clap. The dogs barked louder, and the sailor on duty in the boiler room at the cannery blew the steam whistle. That sent birds off for miles around.

Miss Etheridge was trying to smile up at us and at the same time keep her balance in the rocking boat. She was flustered, her face as red as some of the wilting flowers Char was holding.

One of the sailors in the honor guard said, "She looks scared to death."

The one next to him added, "Yeh, and wait 'til she sees Sedluk. She'll fly back to Dutch Harbor on her own power." That got a laugh.

Lieutenant McCall turned to stare at them with gravedigger eyes. By then, some sailors had lifted her up from the whaleboat and were helping her on the ladder. Rain galoshes aren't made for climbing, and I doubt she'd ever come up four feet of dock ladder hand over hand.

"Tenshun," shouted the end man of the honor guard, and they presented arms as she stepped over the edge. She had thin legs, like reeds.

She was surprised at the guns and almost lost her balance. Later, we laughed about it—what would have happened if she'd gone backward and splashed in; the lieutenant and sailors diving after her.

Tufts of light brown hair stuck out from beneath the fur hat, and we could see a pink scarf at her collar. She had an alligator skin pocketbook and carried an umbrella hooked over one arm. She looked a little old-fashioned.

Except for one thing, Miss Sarah Etheridge, was as plain as a scrubbed new potato, one with a small mouth and small pointed nose. It was her eyes. They jumped out. I'd never seen such clear blue eyes. Blue as an iceberg with sun behind it. Yet they didn't seem cold.

Lieutenant McCall shouted, "Welcome to Sedluk," so everyone on shore could hear him. There was more clapping. He moved up to her, escorted her past the honor guard and then stopped again.

Introducing himself as "Commander, Naval Communications Station," as well as "mayor of Sedluk," he told her how everyone had been waiting months for this day. He went on and on in that booming voice while she stood fidgeting, now and then glancing toward shore, smiling nervously.

When he finished, Miss Etheridge made a speech, too, but not many people heard it. Her voice was too thin. She said she hoped she'd be a good teacher and looked forward to meeting everyone in the settlement. There wasn't much chance she wouldn't.

Lieutenant McCall signaled for Char to present the flowers and then escorted Miss Etheridge off the dock, introducing her to us as he passed. All I said was "Hello," wondering if she'd load on the homework.

On the beach, the lieutenant took her down the line of parents and smaller children and finally walked her to the teacher's quarters, a one-bedroom house about midway along the shore houses.

There'd been a special mother's committee working on it for almost a month, putting "feminine paint," as my mother called it, over the light gray government issue. They'd drawn curtains and linens from the

Supply Department and cooked enough food to last her several weeks. We trailed along until her door was closed and then went up to the cannery to wait for the mail to be sorted.

As Yeoman Second Boyle, the second-class clerk, stacked up letters, magazines and parcels by family, I commented, "Miss Etheridge looks like a bird with blue eyes."

Tony grinned back. "Miss Partridge."

That was it, she was a reed-legged partridge.

Even Max Unger, waiting with us, laughed.

Char didn't think it was funny, though, and told Tony, "You do anything mean to her, and I'll . . ."

Yeoman Boyle said, "Hey, kids, knock it off."

But that's how Miss Etheridge got her nickname the day she arrived.

Now that Miss Etheridge was there and settling in, I felt I could get back to more important things. I was still very angry with Baku since he had what was left of Vulcan. I thought I might be able to take it over to Unigak and have "Chips," the station carpenter, cut out a new stock for it on the band saw.

But I was worried about getting it back from the old man, so I put some tobacco in a piece of cloth and went up to the ridge about five o'clock, knowing he'd be back from the river cut and plain. I put the cloth in my pocket so it wouldn't be obvious that I had it.

I stood outside and called for him, shouting above the dog yaps. Soon the old man came out. He squinted at me and for a moment I thought I saw a crinkling around his eyes, almost a smile. Then he went back inside.

I felt my stomach fall but didn't have the courage to go up and knock on his door. That story about his killing a man in the Aleutians had always bothered me. I stood there maybe a half minute and then decided I'd have to tell my father what had really happened. Maybe he could get Vulcan back.

I turned away and started down the ridge again. I'd gone about fifty feet when I heard him shout, "Hello!"

I stopped and looked back. He was outside the hut, holding Vulcan. I could see there was a stock on it now. I went closer to him, and he held the gun out but seemed to be pretending I wasn't even there. His eyes studied the dogs.

I took the gun and thanked Baku. It was a beautiful, hand-carved stock. He'd done it in only two or three days. It looked better than the original.

I said, "Baku, I want to be friends again."

He gave a half shrug, nodded very slightly, and then examined me closely, scanning for a pocket bulge. "You bring tobacco?" he asked.

I laughed at him. "Yes, Baku, I brought tobacco." I gave him the small packet, and he stuffed it away without a word. Then he cocked his head toward the stock. "You rub bear grease," he said. "Two, three days."

"I will, Baku. It's a fine stock."

The old man seemed embarrassed and stared again at the dogs. I had to move around to see his eyes. I asked, "All right if I go with you in the morning? I won't bring the gun."

What might have been another smile passed quickly around the wrinkled skin beneath the deep holes. He said, "You bring gun," and went inside.

We hunted together for another three or four days. Then Baku, smelling winter in the air, began to complain of boneaches. He said he wanted to sleep for a week and sent me away.

[2]

Already, the sun was thin and hazy. Far north and east, the ice had started sailing slowly toward us, a silent white fleet that would surround Unigak Island and push into the strait in November. We had begun to race against the bad weather.

My mother was canning the last of the garden vegetables; making jellies and jams from the late summer wild berries. The kitchen was steamy and sweet with the smells of boiling pots. Mason jars lined up in a parade of deep cherry and green and yellow. My mother had been a country girl and knew how to preserve things.

On his time off from Unigak, my father was tending the smoker in the back yard where fish were turning a nutty brown. He'd already smoked more than fifty fat salmon. Some would be Christmas gifts for the States.

While waiting for school to start, I helped them. I

also shot goals over in the cannery with Tony and worked with Max sorting some quartz he'd picked up back in the mountains. None of us saw much of Char Midgett. She was following Miss Etheridge around like a calf at feeding time.

One day, I helped bring desks and books and paper from the cannery up to the school, towing them up the muddy road on a big work sled behind one of the small tractors. I talked to Miss Etheridge for a while after we got the books and paper sorted.

"You know, ever since I was a little girl and read about the wilderness in books I've wanted to come to some place like this."

"Didn't you like San Francisco?"

"Yes, very much. It's just that I've never traveled before. You don't know how lucky you are."

I said I thought that I did. Then I asked her, "How would you like to go hunting?"

She smiled and shook her head. "I don't like to see animals killed. I don't see how anyone can shoot them just for sport."

"How about for food?"

"That's a little different," she replied. "But if you'd like to take me out sometime and show me the game . . ."

"I'm a hunter," I said, and that was that.

On September 12, school began. Almost everyone in Sedluk turned out again. This time, it was to watch Miss Etheridge pull the rope on a big brass bell in the schoolyard. No one knew exactly how that bell got to Sedluk from the Navy Yard down in Bremerton, Washington. But it was ours.

It was mounted on a stand that had been welded together over on Unigak. It shined so you could see your face in it, and your nose looked as big as a turnip. The name of a ship was engraved on it and the bell rope was braided.

In midsummer, after he put it up, my father chuckled over that bell. He said it was "obtained" by a chief machinist friend of his who knew a bosun's mate who knew how to get it on a seaplane without anyone looking. And that's how it got to Sedluk. Later, he told an entirely different story, saying that the bell was donated and not swiped. Whatever, a ship named *Edgerton* was minus its bell.

Miss Etheridge rang the *Edgerton* bell, and it echoed back to the mountains. Lieutenant McCall made another speech that sounded as if we were dedicating a bridge to the moon instead of a boxy wooden building. Then we all went inside. Sedluk Settlement School was officially in session.

It had one big room, with a drumlike oil stove in the right-hand corner, a broom and storage closet along the left wall. A girls' and boys' bathroom was attached to the left side. The whole front wall was covered with blackboards. The room smelled of fresh paint and floor wax.

There were twenty desks, and on each one Miss Etheridge had put a slip of paper with the name of a student, older ones grouped in the back. The eight to elevens sat in the middle of the room, and the six to eights up front. That's the way she was going to teach us. We pledged allegiance to the flag and then sat down, waiting for our "Miss Partridge" to say something.

She'd dressed up for the occasion. She seemed very excited, shining as much as the *Edgerton* bell. That first day, I remember, she wore a crinkly white cloth flower on her blue polka-dot dress. Her brown hair was done up.

The first thing she wrote on the blackboard was "Give of yourself." She read it off to the little ones and then to us. "Now, that's what I expect of all of you. To give of yourselves, to study hard and make a contribution to the school."

She went on, "Imagine that our school is a ship, and that we are on a voyage to seek knowledge, and each book is a port of call."

I glanced over at Tony DiSantis, and we both sighed.

It was going to be a long, dreadful time before spring came again.

I didn't really mean to get off on the wrong foot with Miss Etheridge, but going to school the second morning I saw the Midgetts' two bird dogs raising a ruckus back on the tundra a couple of hundred yards from the road.

They'd chased a wandering snowshoe hare into a burrow that had been blocked off by one of the poles carrying electric wire from the cannery to the school. He was in there not more than a foot and a half. The dogs were yapping and trying to dig him out. I pushed them away and then reached in to grab him behind the neck. He came out scratching, scared to death. He wasn't very big.

I thought I might show him to Miss Etheridge, so I tucked him inside my skin parka and went on to school. He quieted down. They'll quiet down if you rub them just behind the ears and hide their heads from light.

I didn't take off my parka, and Tony spotted the bulge.

"Old tundra hare," I told him.

We'd already pledged allegiance, and Miss Etheridge was starting the six to eights on alphabets when Tony whispered, "Why don't you turn him loose?"

That wasn't a bad idea, I thought, so I pulled him out of the parka and put him down on the floor. He took off for the front of the room as if his tail was burning. He ran into the front wall wide open, tumbled back, and took off again.

Miss Etheridge screamed. She threw her hands up and jumped three feet as the hare skidded between the desks. The little ones up front screamed, too, until they saw what it was.

It took Tony and me three or four minutes to get him in a corner where we could grab him. I carried him outside by his hind legs and let him loose. He scampered off toward the ridge.

Miss Etheridge was standing behind her desk when I entered, her face red, her eyes sparking. She looked straight at me and asked, "Did you do that, Dory?"

I nodded.

"Then you can march right out of here and go home."

I said, "Yes, m'am."

As I was getting my books from under my desk, she said, "If you don't tell your mother what happened, I will."

I nodded again.

As I was leaving, she said, "While you're home today, you can write 'Animals belong outdoors' one thousand times."

I went on home. After that, we never really got along too well.

Winter arrived September 20.

There was a grayness in the sky, and the wind moaned. The sun was blurred at noon, and Unigak Bay was covered with spurting whitecaps. About four o'clock, the snow flew down from the north in teasing flurries.

It wasn't a bad storm, but the tundra froze temporarily that day, so that it felt like leather under your feet. There were patches of thin ice around now, and the brown ground looked as though it had been sprinkled with powdered sugar.

We took our caribou parkas and pants down from the closets and tried them on again. Most of the families had bought them in Kotzebue, along with fur boots, because they were much warmer than anything we'd brought from the States.

When the first snow fell, I went out to the pen.

Netsig was sitting up, his nose pointed to the sky as though he was smelling some good, familiar scent.

I tried not to worry about him, since his coat would keep him warm even if the temperature dropped to forty below. It seldom got that cold on Unigak Bay, I was told.

Netsig could hobble along at a fair pace now and was even trying to run. With the leg almost healed, he could put a little weight on it. Yet the first time I saw him try to run, I didn't know whether to laugh or cry. His left hip went up and down like a loose piston rod.

I knew that he couldn't outrun the game back on the plain or in the valley, so I watched that he didn't go back there. And I had still another worry. Someone might shoot him, not realizing he was a pet.

The third week in September I went out to the island. The boat coxswain, an expert in rope and leather, helped me fashion a wide collar for him. No hunter, I thought, would fire at a wolf with a collar around his neck. Netsig didn't like it very much, but it had to be on him when he wasn't penned.

It thawed for a few days after the first flurries of snow, but then the temperature dropped again. The tundra froze hard all the way down to the permanent ice layer below. What would hit us from now on would be storms so fierce that the snow would look as though it were smoking; dunes of blowing snow.

Again, I fought the temptation to bring Netsig inside. My father flatly refused even to consider it. Curled up like Baku's dogs, head pointed away from the wind, he'd be as warm as we were. But sometimes it was hard to believe that. At night, when the wind would howl, I'd think of him outside.

There was less daylight each day, and I didn't go near Baku's after the hard freeze. I went to school six days a week and spent most of the afternoons working on model airplanes. I had seven kits saved up for the winter; Navy planes like the Wildcat fighter, the King-fisher float plane and the big Catalina seaplane. I listened to radio a lot. To "The Saint" and "Charlie Chan," which were mystery shows; "Amos n' Andy," a comedy show, and "Fred Waring," which was a band. Saturday nights, we'd all go to the cannery building to watch a movie on the sixteen-millimeter projector. No one ever missed that. Sometimes we'd run them again Sunday afternoon.

But time passed slowly once the arctic night shut down on us completely in early November. Since the days were so short, we'd go to school and return in darkness. If there was a heavy storm, we'd stay home. The men on Unigak would not even cross over, though the ice was now solid to the shore. They could be lost a few hundred feet from their buildings. But they had plenty of food, and we could talk to them by phone.

Miss Etheridge seemed very lonely at times, al-though we included her in everything we did in the settlement. It was just that she'd always end up the day by herself. Lights would go on in her small house, but we knew she had no one to talk to. Only her stacks of books to read.

None of the single enlisted men seemed interested

in her. Certainly, the Eskimos weren't interested. They liked their women plumper, my father said.

One night he said, "May as well face it, Miss Etheridge is doomed to be a spinster."

My mother bristled. "You might have been doomed to be a bachelor if I hadn't come along."

[3]

Miss Etheridge did try to teach us a lot of things. About a week before Thanksgiving, she decided to have "Eskimo Day" at the school. She thought we didn't really know too much about them; that we took them for granted the way they were. In a way, she was right.

She began gathering everything Eskimo that she could find. She borrowed carved walrus tusks and an old birdskin hat from Mrs. Thorkilsen. The Bering Sea Eskimos had been the best ivory carvers; the birdskin hat came from the Nushagagmiuts.

From Mrs. Thorkilsen, she also got wooden tribal masks and knives, including an old *ulu* (which is a woman's knife), a bark peeler and a flint flaker with an antelope handle. Mrs. Thorkilsen said to be careful with them because they should be in that museum they were talking about building in Anchorage.

Max Unger collected some things like arrowheads and harpoon heads and brought them to school. I thought about going up to Baku's and asking to borrow his bows and whale and seal harpoons and his odd-looking fishing nets. But, knowing him, I decided against it.

Miss Etheridge decided we must have a speaker, and Mrs. Thorkilsen suggested Nante. He'd gone to one of the federal schools when he was young, and his English was as good as anyone's. Nante had a small office in the cannery and bossed the other Eskimos in maintenance work.

For a while, some of the mothers had tried to pair Nante and Miss Etheridge, especially after the Halloween social when she flopped with the younger single men from Unigak. But Nante had an Eskimo girl at Kotzebue and didn't see much in Miss Etheridge and her reed legs.

Nante said he'd be delighted to talk to the children about Eskimos and came up the road that day carrying an old Armour's lard tin. We all wondered what was in it.

To start off, Miss Etheridge asked him about the tribes along the Bering Coast. Nante answered that they were mostly Nushagagmiut or Algemiut but that none of the Eskimos around Sedluk were purebred from either tribe. Proudly, he said he was the only real Eskimo there: an authentic Togiakmiut from Bristol Bay.

Then Char asked where the Eskimos came from originally.

Nante's eyes lit up. "From Raven, a great bird that flew to earth from out of heaven."

One of the little ones up front asked, "Did God send him down?"

Nante replied flatly, "No, he came down by himself!" Then he went on, "When he flew down, he carried beach peas in his beak, and these he planted the first day on earth. After the sun went south and came north again, out of one pea pod came a man."

Max Unger's little sister said, "That was Adam!"

"No," Nante said, "that was the first Eskimo, and then Raven took his feathers off, and removed his beak and became a man, too, with hands and feet. That was so he could make animals out of clay. After he made the animals—caribou and moose and mountain sheep— he made fish. Now, there would be plenty of food, so from another pea pod he made a woman."

"That was Eve," the Unger girl said.

Nante looked at her, a bit annoyed. But he answered, "That was the first Eskimo woman."

"Children, please don't interrupt," Miss Etheridge said.

Nante flashed a smile at her and continued, "The man then made the mountains by pushing with his hands, and he scratched his head on them to make the forests, so the animals could live there. The woman, on the other hand, urinated to make the seas, and then began spitting on the land to make the lakes, and from them the rivers flowed."

I remember there wasn't a sound in the room. Not even a cough. I shot a glance at Char. Her face was red, but not as red as Miss Etheridge's. I looked up at Nante. There were crinkles of a devil around his dark eyes.

"So the woman and the man bore children, and then

Raven sent them off, some to the Arctic, some to the mountains; some were left here along the coast. That's why we have Arctic tribes, inland tribes and coast tribes like my own Togiak."

After another silence, Char asked, "Who made the sun and the moon and the stars, if Raven did all those other things?"

Nante said, "Raven did! He knew the Eskimos, to be able to hunt and provide food for the winter, had to have some light. He changed himself into a bird again and flew back to heaven. Millions of miles away, there was a hot ball of rock in the sky. He towed it closer to where the Eskimos were living and called it the sun."

"What about the moon?" someone asked.

"Raven realized that the Eskimos could not hunt the way they should without sleep. So he went back to heaven and found a smaller ball of rock that was not hot and didn't glow. That became the moon so the Eskimos could sleep better."

"The stars," Char said determinedly.

"I don't know," Nante answered, "but Raven certainly made them."

For the next twenty minutes he answered questions, especially about where Raven had obtained those original pea pods in heaven. He said Raven had some secrets that he didn't tell anyone.

At last, he looked at his watch and said that he would soon have to go back to the cannery building but wanted to give us a treat. He drew some paper plates out of a bag and began to ladle spoons of a yellowish-gray mass out of the lard tin. Smiling widely, he said, "*Akotuk*. It is Eskimo ice cream but not like yours."

I glanced over at Max. We'd had it before. It sure wasn't like ours. It was dried meat and mashed caribou tallow.

He passed the plates around and then watched as everybody tried to get it down. Miss Etheridge was a little green, but she finished hers.

Then Nante reached into the paper bag again and drew out a handful of small gray wads about the size of hickory nuts. "Put them in your mouths. It is Eskimo chewing gum."

Miss Etheridge examined hers and asked, "How is it made?"

Nante smiled. "Congealed seal oil and willow catkins."

Miss Etheridge murmured weakly, "Oh," and closed those blue eyes before putting the gray wad in her mouth.

A few minutes later, she thanked Nante for visiting the school. He said he'd be glad to come back any time.

He wasn't more than a few hundred yards down the dark road when the whole class emptied out. Everyone went outside either to get some air or to throw up in the new snow.

Eskimo Day had ended.

Miss Etheridge let us out of school for a week at Thanksgiving. The middle and older children spent most of it tobogganing on the high ridge. We made a fast run for the older children and a slow one for the middles.

Those days were magic, I remember, with kerosene flares burning on the slope and down it, like huge, bright flickering candles. They cast a merry glow in the dark against the whiteness of the snow. It did not matter that day was night. The whole ridge echoed with shouts and laughter.

For Thanksgiving, food was brought up from our cold storage under the back porch and thawed. We had one of the big swans, with a sweet root-and-celery dressing. My mother said we didn't need it, but my father hacksawed a piece of caribou roast, and we had that, too.

There was no place on the table that wasn't covered with a dish. All the colors of the rainbow spread across it, and steam shimmered up from the platters, mingling the meat and berry and vegetable smells.

My father bent his head in prayer. "Oh, Lord, we thank Thee for all the bountiful gifts from the land around us. We thank Thee for the love, peace and happiness of our home."

It was a true statement that day.

[4]

Then, suddenly, it was Sunday, December 7, 1941.

I don't know that it was exactly an honor, but Sedluk was one of the first places in the world to hear about

Pearl Harbor. The Unigak radio operator on the eight-to-twelve watch that morning monitored the broadcast that said, "Air Raid, Pearl Harbor! This is no drill!"

He telephoned Lieutenant McCall, who was home in Sedluk, and the word spread quickly. We couldn't believe it, at first. Japan had attacked the United States, bombing the naval base in Honolulu.

The adults seemed worried. Unigak Bay was almost as close to Japan as it was to Washington. Besides our hunting guns, there were only the drill and sentry rifles, which hadn't been used since the honor guard saluted Miss Etheridge the day she arrived.

There were a few Army troops at Nome, we'd heard; some in Juneau, Cold Bay and Cordova. There were Army Air Corps planes at Ladd Field, at Elmendorf and Yakutat and maybe at some other places we didn't know about. The Navy had those patrol planes at Dutch Harbor, but in winter they weren't of much use in far north waters. They couldn't land on ice.

Everyone came out of the houses, and we stood in the dark, snowbound street and talked. Lieutenant McCall put Unigak on an alert, and all the men crossed over to report to duty.

I went to Tony's house with Max Unger and Char. We talked in "ifs." What we'd do *if* the Japanese invaded Sedluk; *if* they bombed us.

Little ax-faced Tony was always belligerent and talked that way now. Max discussed strategy. *If* the war lasted more than four years, Max and I would go—Max into the hospital corps; I'd be a carrier pilot.

If the war lasted five years, Char would be a nurse and Tony a Marine.

During the afternoon, Lieutenant McCall got everyone together in the old church and said we should remain calm. The Japanese couldn't attack us during the winter this far north; they couldn't cross the ice pack. Nor would they risk an invasion force in bad weather for so small a target. We could forget about bombings, he said.

None of the men questioned him, of course, but Mrs. Thorkilsen got up to ask why there had to be a blackout if it was impossible for the Japanese to invade or bomb.

The lieutenant frowned and thought a moment. Then he gave a hollow laugh and sighed. "You're right, Mrs. Thorkilsen. Forget the blackout."

The next day, after we listened to President Roosevelt declare war on Japan, things got back to normal, except that there was much more traffic on the radio channels at Unigak and all the watches were doubled.

My father was really itching to get on a ship and into the fighting. The fourth day after war was declared, he sent a message to Washington again requesting assignment to the carrier *Yorktown*. While he liked living in Sedluk, he wanted sea duty.

Even though he'd never had much schooling, he knew all the stories about John Paul Jones, the first Navy hero, and Captain Lawrence, of USS *Chesapeake*, and "Don't give up the ship."

The day he sent the message he told us, "There's

only one reason for a military man to exist, an' that's to go to war."

My mother asked, "Jake, you ever been to war?"

He got a little flushed and answered, "You know I was too young to get into World War I."

She said, "You just may change your mind."

My father snorted. "You wait 'til I get on the *Yorktown*. I'll find some way o' gettin' my hands on an anti-aircraft gun."

My mother snorted right back. "I know as well as you do that your place is in the radio room, not out shootin' any gun."

He got very angry, and I didn't blame him.

She always nettled him about things like this. She'd grumble when he said he hoped I'd be a Navy pilot. And I don't think she liked it too much when he took me aboard the *Yorktown* while we were stationed in Norfolk. Or out to the air station to watch the Dauntless dive bombers fly away.

He'd look at the planes, shake his head and say, "Sure wish I was your age, boy."

Sometimes when they'd come streaking down the runway, spitting blue flames from the exhaust stacks, he'd yell as if to get in tune with the screaming engine. There would be a fierce look on his craggy face. He wanted to be in the cockpit, but of course he was too old.

That was in '39, the year some friends and I used to fight rowboats down on Paradise Creek, near Portsmouth. After school, if the tide was high enough, we'd maneuver around the reeds and then ram each other broadside, fighting hand-to-hand. We were making believe we were destroyers out in the English Channel.

One late fall afternoon, I remember my father standing on the bank, a grin on his face as he watched us fight. I'll never forget his raising a fist into the air and shouting, "Damn the torpedoes, full speed ahead!"

So it was hard for me to understand why my mother and Miss Etheridge were so much against the war. Miss Etheridge let us talk about it for a day or two after December 7, but then said we had more important things to do in school. Toward the end of that week, I held my hand up one morning and asked her a question.

She looked at me a long time before answering. "I'm against all wars. I'm against our men being killed. I'm against the Japanese being killed, Dory. I'm against innocent people suffering."

"But the Japanese bombed us," I said.

"I know we have to fight back, but I think we should try to end the war through diplomacy. I don't believe in fighting."

That night I told my father that Miss Etheridge was against the war, because that's the way she sounded. I told him she wouldn't let us talk about it.

My father said sharply, "Say that again!"

I repeated it. Everything she'd said.

A little later, my father talked to Lieutenant McCall, and then I suppose he called or went to see Miss Etheridge. Next day in school, she avoided my eyes. When school was over, she asked me to stay a moment. When everyone else was out of the room, she said, her face very grave, "I don't know what you told your father, or what your father told Lieutenant McCall, but I want you to know, Dory, that I am not unpatriotic. I love my country just as much as you do. But I also have my own beliefs."

I didn't say anything. And my mind wasn't changed. She was against the war. She'd said it. I asked if I could go. She nodded, a hurt look on her face. I felt those blue eyes in my back as I went out into the darkness.

[5]

One Sunday a week later, Char and I bummed a ride on a tractor going out to Unigak. We'd always wanted to climb The Foot, the high pinnacle, when snow was on it. So we rigged a rope and stuck nails into the ends of broomsticks to use as pikes, like a movie on mountain climbing that we'd seen.

We'd climbed it during the summer, of course. It was a good place to go. You could sit up there and see for miles around. There were birds' nests, and wild flowers grew out of crevices. The time we'd climbed it in the summer, low clouds came in and foamed around us.

It was, we thought, like being in the Alps, with all of Switzerland spread out below us.

Twilight would last about an hour, just enough for us to get to the peak and back. So we started out an hour ahead of twilight, which was about noon, and walked across the snow to the base of The Foot. Behind us, the station buildings were spooky in the thin pink and blue light.

We tied ourselves together with the ropes and then made a big thing of climbing the slender peak, the way we'd seen the Swiss men in the movie do it.

When we got to the top, we yodeled for a little while, listening to our voices strike up against Sedluk Ridge. We could easily see the radio station, almost snow-buried, smoke curling from stacks on the buildings. One of the men came outside and waved to us.

After a lunch of deer steak slices on homemade bread, thick and soft, we started down again, not using the rope, this time slipping and sliding over the snow, going from shelf to shelf. It was more fun coming down than going up.

But about midway down The Foot, I hit an ice ridge that was barely covered from the last storm. Wind had blown all but an inch or two of snow away. I turned into a human sled for a few seconds, ending up in a drift about fifty feet below, laughing after the surprise of it was over.

Char came down, looked at me, and then said, "You have blood on your leg."

I had felt a sharp pain during the fall, but it didn't amount to much. I looked down at my pants. There was a large rip in them. The ice had also jagged through my heavy underwear.

"It's just a scratch," I said.

"We'd better fix it," Char replied.

"Wait until we get back."

But she insisted, lifting up her parka to rip a piece of cloth from somewhere beneath. It looked like part of her blouse. She sat down beside me and pulled the pants leg further open. Then she peeled the underwear leg back and tried to wrap the cloth over the wound.

She said, "Let's pretend we're in Corregidor, that fort in the Philippines, and I'm a nurse."

I laughed at her. Neither of us had played any "pretend" game in a long time. But I saw she was serious.

She said, "Just close your eyes. You're a soldier, and you've been shot by the Japanese."

"Char, for Pete's sake," I said.

"Close your eyes," she demanded.

So I closed them. There I was, sitting in the snow, getting very cold, and she was telling me to pretend I was in the tropics. If she didn't look out, her hands would be frostbitten in a moment.

She said quietly, "You threw a grenade at them and captured a whole platoon."

I could feel her tugging the cloth around the leg inside the skin pants.

She said, "I don't think we'll have to perform surgery on this. The bullet just grazed you."

I laughed at her.

She said, "Hold still, Major Scofield."

I said, "C'mon, Char, this is nutty."

There was something weird about it. But not nutty; not funny. Suddenly, my throat felt dry.

I opened my eyes just as she was knotting the

rag, doing a very expert job. "There," she said, lifting her head. Then an odd look came over her face.

We stared at each other a moment, and I had that feeling, too, almost as if it had really happened; that bullet *had* grazed me; I *had* been wounded.

Maybe we were frightened by the thought.

Finally, she said, "Don't you think we should go?"

Only a few minutes of the pink-blue light remained. We went down The Foot, not saying anything much. When we reached the station, about a half mile away, one of the enlisted men put a regular bandage on my leg. It was only a deep scratch.

Char and I never talked about that day on The Foot again.

[6]

School let out a week before Christmas, and that was the week of our longest nights. From about the eighteenth through the twenty-first, the day of the winter equinox, there was no light at all. Then on December 22, the sun started its way north again. But at noon that day it was still like midnight.

The next day my father and I put on snowshoes and got an ax and a rope ready for the trip back into the valley to find a small spruce that wasn't buried too deep. In some places, where the snow had drifted, we knew it would be eight to ten feet deep.

We were about the last ones to get our "home" tree.

The main tree for Sedluk had been cut weeks before by the enlisted men and tractored out of the valley. It now stood thirty feet high in the church-yard, colored lights on almost every branch.

The men on boiler duty in the cannery would come out every day or so to knock snow off, leaving just enough to glisten in the reflection of the lights.

Each night, everyone in Sedluk would sit in their front windows and look out at it. At this time, I think we were all trying to forget that there was a war. But the radio reminded us.

I'd asked my father if I could take Netsig with us, and he said that was all right. My father said he'd take his rifle. Anytime anyone went out on the plain or back up in the valley, they knew to carry a gun, especially in the winter. The game had to hunt extra hard for food then. If you hurt yourself, a roving pack of starved wolves could have an unexpected meal.

I also asked my father if I could take Baku a Christmas present since we'd be going that way.

"Fine," he said. "What you gonna give that ol' coot?"

Without thinking, I replied, "Tobacco."

He looked at me for a long time, his eyes narrow and things spinning in his head. Then he laughed. "Well, I'll be damned. If it wasn't Christmas, boy, I'd take you into the bedroom and tan your setter."

I suppose my face was crimson. I know guilt was plastered across it. Since last June, of course, I'd been swiping the burley mix to give to old Baku. It was the only way I could be sure of getting him in the mood to let me go along with him.

My father dug out two tins of Prince Albert, which he didn't like, presents from one of the enlisted men the year before, and my mother wrapped them, putting on a fancy bow.

My father said that was a waste, but I knew it wasn't. Baku found a use for everything he got. After he traded the Prince Albert tins to the other Eskimos, he'd do something with the paper and ribbons.

We went by Baku's, my father holding Netsig on a rope about two hundred yards away from the hut so that the sled dogs wouldn't get upset. But they did anyway. They roused out of their snow beds and made a terrible fuss while I was knocking on Baku's door.

His hut actually had two rooms. One was a large room in which he slept and ate; the other a smaller entrance room like our enclosed back porch where he took off his heavy trail clothes, and stored his guns, harpoons and traps. Aside from the yellow gleam of the blubber lamp, it was always dark inside Baku's hut.

I was glad that the dogs were yowling because it took forever to awaken him. He finally came out, blinking, frowning and scratching himself. He was wearing something like a deer hide turned inside out. I guess it was his indoor underwear. I doubt if he'd opened that door for weeks because the odor that came out would have brought a moose to its knees.

I shouted, "Merry Christmas," and gave him the package.

He frowned at it, shook it hard, and then closed the door and went back inside without uttering a word. I don't think he even knew what month it was.

My father roared with laughter because he could read the disappointment on my face.

I said, "I'll never give him anything else."

My father choked back his laughter to say, "Not the spirit, boy."

We crossed the plain, Netsig moving at a half trot, using his bad leg as though he were kicking a scooter along. We'd taken him off the rope, and he was weaving a figure-eight pattern out in front of us.

His coat had turned a wintry gray and must have been two inches thick. Except for that gimpy leg, he was powerful now, and weighed around ninety pounds. He was a handsome dog. I seldom thought of him as a wolf.

Midway across, he stumbled on a big snowshoe rabbit and tried to chase him. After a few seconds, I turned my head away. His left flank went up and down in a pathetically clumsy motion.

My father didn't say anything.

When he came back to us, panting, bushy tail flagging, my father told him, "Keep tryin', you gimp dog."

Big jaws open, teeth shining, eyes asparkle, he seemed to be genuinely grinning, happy to be out on the plain instead of penned up, not fretting at all because he'd lost that upstart rabbit. Ice was beginning to form in little clumps under his whiskery belly.

My father was in a good mood, singing now and then, probably thinking about the Carolina highlands and galax and holly as we shuffled down the slope into the valley. He was a Roan Mountain man and had done this as a little boy.

The river was frozen solid, of course, and snow covered. Drifts had piled along the south shore and in some places only the very tops of the stubby birches were sticking out. But the wind that often sliced up the valley had whisked away most of the snow on the north bank. It was only a few feet deep there, so we stuck to that side.

We got back to the spruce stand and found a nice one. It was about seven feet tall, a perfect upside down V and thick with needles. My father pounded the base of it to knock most of the snow off, then cut it, ax blows ringing in the still air.

He had rigged a loop for his shoulder and tied the rope to it so he could drag the tree over the snow. It was like powder and dry, but had a good base.

We'd only gotten a hundred feet or so from the stand when he stopped and said, "You know, view of what's happened, I think it might be a good idea for you to take that teacher a tree."

"Mother took her over two eiders, a reindeer roast and some currant jelly yesterday," I said, avoiding the other issue.

Miss Etheridge and I had argued right along. She was still dead against the war, didn't like guns of any kind and thought hunters were terrible people.

"Never mind, let's cut a bitty one for her."

So we went back and got one about four feet high. I dragged it while he pulled the big one. Going up the slope was rough, but after that it was downhill all the way to Sedluk.

We were both pretty tired by the time we got home, but I went over to Miss Etheridge's with the tree. Same as I'd done at Baku's, I knocked at her door and said, "Merry Christmas."

She laughed. "What a surprise, Dory!"

I suppose I was blushing, after the trouble we'd had.

She told me to leave the tree on the stoop and made me come in, although I didn't really want to. She'd decorated the little house, and there were lots of presents around. In fact, I'd never seen so much stuff packed into one room. There were sealskin boots and at least two caribou blankets. A seal parka was draped over one chair. It looked like Nante's work.

I guess everybody in Sedluk had given her something except Baku, and he didn't give anybody anything.

I looked out toward the kitchen. There was enough food piled up in there to feed all the Eskimos in Kotzebue.

Miss Etheridge said, "I want to wish you a very Merry Christmas, Dory," and then she gave me a package. By the feel of it, I could tell it was a book.

She leaned forward and kissed my forehead, which I hadn't expected.

Last I saw of her that late afternoon, she was standing on her stoop, framed in the glow of the inside light, looking at the tree and running her finger along her chin thoughtfully.

(It wasn't until well after Christmas that I learned she'd had a big problem with trees. There had been fourteen others, almost one from each student, piled up like cordwood on her back porch. Mine was the last. None of us ever knew which one she put up.)

On Christmas Eve, after having brant eggs and thick crab soup at home, topped off with wild cherry snow cream, we gathered in front of the big tree in the old Russian churchyard and sang carols.

Tucked in fur circles of parkas, all the faces were shining. The voices, sharp and clear, seemed to go back endlessly into the cold reaches of the plain. I stood by my mother and father singing, and truly, there did not seem to be a war anywhere.

After five carols, Nante did a dance before the tree. He was waving what appeared to be a seal's bladder hanging from a stick. He danced in a circle and shouted something like "hoi, hoi, hoi," while one of the other Eskimos beat two pieces of whalebone together. I didn't think it was much of a Christmas dance, but everybody applauded.

Nante had done it to give Lieutenant McCall a chance to go behind the church and pull on a Santa Claus suit that the Navy Supply Corps in Seattle had sent, along with bags of hard candy for all the children.

In a moment, he came out from behind the church driving Nante's dog team, shouting, "Merry Christmas." It ended in kind of a mess when he tried to turn the huskies and fell off the sled. But nobody minded.

Then Mrs. Thorkilsen sang "Silent Night, Holy Night," in her alto voice, and it *was* that kind of a still, pure night. When she had finished, there were shouts of Merry Christmas again, and we went home, just crossing the street.

In the morning, Miss Etheridge's package was one of the first I opened. It was *Lives of Game Animals*, by Ernest Thompson Seton, a famous book I heard later.

[7]

Near the end of January (now 1942) we first saw real light after our days of twilight and darkness. Around noon, there was a glow where the velvet sky and the earth separated. Each day that glow became stronger as the ribbon of sun widened.

Then one day, the sun returned for just a few moments, and we saw the full, warm ball of it. Everyone in Sedluk ran up to the ridge to watch just as long as they could, shouting and dancing about. The sun had returned to our cold, blue world and we knew that in a few weeks spring would come.

But as if to remind us that it would be back, winter provided a final storm the first and second of

March, a mean howler of icy wind that drove snow before it, gusting and rattling our house. Then it withdrew, leaving a painted blue sky in late morning. Soon, the sea began to open up, ice cracking into floes as it started its slow, majestic voyage north again.

We followed the war from Anchorage radio, and from the "newspaper," a mimeographed daily bulletin Lieutenant McCall put together over on Unigak and posted in the cannery. Our ships were being sunk around the world; Wake Island had been captured. They said it was only a matter of time until our Army and Navy surrendered in the Philippines. The enemy was winning.

Now, with the ice departing, we wondered if the Japanese might decide to attack Alaska. But no one talked about it much. Miss Etheridge had gotten so she would not even mention the war. She simply closed her ears to it.

A few weeks later, spring arrived.

There were patches of brown all over the plain and on the stretch of tundra between the shore houses and the high ridge. The frost coating on the ceiling of our back porch had disappeared, and our road was muddy again.

If you went up to the plain and stood very still, you could hear the land melting. In winter, the tundra moss lies between the snow and the frozen ground. Now, it was alive with moist growth. The brown roots were turning yellow and the grass had fresh catkins on it. You could see spiders on the white lichen. They had survived the winter.

The first flowers we saw were rose colored and lavender. Soon, yellow poppies would be mounded everywhere on the plain. Within a few weeks, there would be miles of waving beds and fields of reds and blues and golds; wild geraniums, dandelions, daisies with black eyes the size of quarters.

The late spring and summer fogs that occasionally wrapped Sedluk like steel wool were a month away, so the village was sprayed in bright sunlight. It looked clean and washed after the winter storms.

Baku had started hunting again; this time, for seals. When he was a younger man, I'm sure he had hunted them on the ice, waiting quietly at their breathing holes to drive a harpoon into them. But ice hunting was too difficult for him now so he was seeking them in the offshore rocks when they'd come out to bask.

We launched the kayaks and went south of Unigak to a low cropping of rocks about two miles offshore. I did not bring Vulcan along because I was afraid of dropping it overboard. Also, there was nothing to shoot at except birds. You don't shoot seals with a shotgun, my father said. I didn't know much about it. I'd never been on a seal hunt.

Baku, of course, had his 30.30 and a harpoon with a bladder float attached to it. While my kayak dipped a little from side to side as I paddled it, Baku's stayed almost completely level. He paddled almost soundlessly, and his blade hardly dripped any water. He handled the paddle as if he were sewing in the sea with a long needle. Once, when I splashed, he turned to look back at me, those deep-hole eyes signaling a warning.

As we got close to the rocks, Baku checked his harpoon and bladder float, then began making a bird call to cover our sounds. The seals would not be alarmed if they thought only a bird was approaching.

Baku put his paddle down and held up his hand as if he were a traffic cop. I stopped paddling, and our kayaks glided toward the end of the rocks.

He lifted the harpoon and drew it back.

I saw maybe a dozen bearded seals on the rocks, near the water's edge. The nearest one was a big male, not more than fifteen feet away. He turned his bristly head, but it was too late. Already, the harpoon was making an arc toward him.

As the seal dived into the water, the harpoon blade struck him just below the head. He cried out, and the others hit the water, fanning away and diving to safety. The bladder float flew through the air, its line taut as it followed the seal. Then he disappeared for a few seconds under the water.

Baku was watching for him, and lifted the 30.30 as he popped to the surface again. Suddenly, he swerved toward Baku's kayak, and the old man, sitting calm as the yellow church dome, waved at me to stay clear. He picked up his paddle again.

The big bull seal, enraged at the attack, was out to chew a hole in Baku's kayak. He must have weighed six or seven hundred pounds. You could see him just below the water, his square-flippered, gray-brown body a mass of angry, twisting muscle.

Like a bull fighter facing a charge, Baku waited until the seal was within a few feet of the kayak, the end of the harpoon whipping across the gelid sea. Then he shot the kayak forward as the water swirled beneath him.

The seal turned and charged again, and Baku danced the kayak away with a sweep of paddle, shouting at me to get out of the water.

I headed for the rocks and pulled my kayak out, while Baku turned away from still another attack. I wondered what I could do to help him. Clearly, his life was in danger.

Then, for a moment, the bladder float stayed motionless on the red-frothed surface as if the seal was plotting a final assault.

I watched Baku. He was staring at the bladder, making his own decision. He was between the seal and the rocks. Either could easily punch a hole in the skin of the kayak. He couldn't turn his back on the seal to paddle to the rocks. Yet the only safety was on the rocks. I wished the seal would just swim away.

Suddenly, he charged again, bearing straight into the kayak. It was a killer charge. Baku yelled something in Eskimo, some wild, hoarse cry at the raging seal, and I saw that his leathery face was lit up. For a second, it seemed he was young again.

This time, the bull was only inches from the kayak as Baku spun it like a top, crying out savagely. The seal turned as he lost his target, but Baku had already reached the rocks and with incredible speed had lifted the kayak out.

He gave another cry in Eskimo, a roaring cry of victory. He shook his fist at the seal and picked up the 30.30, sighting toward the bladder.

Another moment passed before the seal stuck his head out of the water to look for the man and kayak. The 30.30 crashed, echoing over the quiet water, and the battle was over. Baku stomped his foot on the rocks and glanced over at me as if to say, *Boy, that is how it was when I was young.*

Then he launched his kayak, went out to the bladder and hauled the seal ashore. He seemed tired now.

There was still a tiny beat of life in the big bull. He was a beautiful animal, and there were scars on his hide just as there were scars on Bakutan's.

I looked into his eyes before the final glaze came over them. There was nothing hateful in them; nothing to tell about the terrible fight he'd had with Baku. They were big and brown and peaceful.

I did not go seal hunting again with Bakutan.

[8]

A few days later, Netsig left me.

I suppose every boy knows that sooner or later his dog will leave. Go off and explore. You always hope they'll come back. Muddy, panting and hungry.

On the morning of May 5, I came out of the house

to see a bulge in the pen wire. I guess he'd pushed up against it long enough to spring it loose.

I looked over the tundra for him and saw nothing. I went through the settlement, end to end, and into every back yard. Then I came home, got Vulcan and went up into the valley, stopping off at Baku's to see if he was home. He'd already gone.

I could find no trace of Netsig in the valley and so searched the south end of the plain until late afternoon. I must have walked twenty miles that day.

In the evening, I sat out in back waiting for him until almost midnight, trying to make myself believe he'd return if he could. I kept seeing him moving around out there on that gimpy leg. I was certain he wouldn't tangle with a wolverine again. But there was other game that could kill a crippled wolf.

My father sat with me for a while. He said, "You knew this might happen, Dory."

I knew it, but that didn't help anything.

Darkness closed in finally, but I didn't get more than a few hours of sleep. Each time a howl would echo down off the ridge I'd get up and look out.

At about 3 A.M., when it was daylight, I fixed some oatmeal with currants and then set off again. During the darkness I had thought about the pinnacles and the dens that were up there. So I went in that direction, searching along them north and west.

I looked in every abandoned lair I could find, under every overhanging rock, calling out for him. I worked steadily toward the one he'd found that first day I had him out. I got there about 5 A.M. There were some tracks around it, and I called for him. No sound came out.

I got down on my hands and knees, looking in. There he was, head between his paws, just like he belonged in that den.

"You dumb dog, you scared me half to death," I said.

I reached in, dug my fingers around his ears and ordered him to come out. He did, stretching lazily, and then shaking himself. I couldn't see a scratch on him. He trotted beside me back to the settlement as if he'd been on a walk down to the school. At home, he had some food and water and went to sleep.

I knew now that Baku and Netsig were part of the land and would never change.

Part III

THE INVADERS

[1]

One morning in early June, just a few days after my thirteenth birthday, we learned that the war had come to the Bering Sea. The Japanese had invaded the islands of Attu and Kiska at the far end of the Aleutians. Then our towers on Unigak picked up a frantic call from Dutch Harbor on the island of Unalaska, even closer to us. The Navy base there was under air attack.

The siren on Unigak sent a chilling wail into the air as Lieutenant McCall ordered an immediate alert, posting guards on the west beach of the island. Everyone came out on the road and Sedluk buzzed. Now, the war was almost on our doorstep.

Before getting in the whaleboat with the other off-duty men to go over to the island my father said, "All right, boy, simmer down, they're still a long way from here. You go to school and go 'bout your chores just the same as yesterday. Help your mother. Let's don't fall apart."

It was almost like that day in December when

we'd heard about Pearl Harbor. Everyone was a little nervous as we watched the whaleboat chug across to the island.

After school, I took Vulcan and my father's two shotguns, and his .305 rifle out in the back yard. Although they were clean, I cleaned and oiled them again. Then I got all of our shotgun shells together and counted them. I did the same with my father's rifle bullets.

My mother came out to ask, "What are you doin', Dory?"

I said I was just cleaning our guns. She frowned at me but didn't say anything. I think she knew what I had on my mind.

But by evening it quieted down. The raid at Dutch Harbor didn't last long, and there wasn't too much damage. Over supper, my father said, "Maybe they're trying to keep us off balance. Make us spread our forces."

I asked what he meant.

"We're starting to concentrate in the mid-Pacific. If the Japs can make us pull ships and men away from there, it takes the pressure off them. It's called a flanking maneuver."

"Can they get away with it?" I asked.

His laugh was strange. "They already have. They're ashore on Kiska and Attu."

After supper, he went out into the front room and sat in his chair. Face glum, he just stared off into space. I didn't try to talk to him. I knew he felt helpless, not being on the *Yorktown*; not even having the luck to be at Dutch Harbor and maybe fire an anti-aircraft gun. Day after day, all he did was listen to messages from Japan, mostly to their ships at sea in northern waters.

The next day, Lieutenant McCall gave up on the idea of sentries on the west beach of Unigak. There weren't enough men to walk patrols and also keep the duty watches at the station. He told everybody that our main responsibility was communications and not combat.

Blinds drawn tight, Sedluk was deep in sleep that midnight when the Japanese struck.

They came in under a patchy fog, landing on the west beach at Unigak. Only one shot was fired over there, and that was an accident involving a nervous Japanese soldier. They simply pushed open the doors to the communications building and lined the six men on duty up against the walls.

A little later, the door to my room flew open, and I saw two small helmeted men in brown uniforms holding rifles with bayonets attached. It wasn't until one of them said something in Japanese that I finally realized who they were.

Funny, earlier in the day I'd thought about this very thing happening and what I'd do. I'd grab Vulcan and start firing. But now I was paralyzed.

One of them barked something that sounded like "Kow-owwww," and nodded his head for me to get out of bed.

From the front room, I heard my father say firmly, "Boy, don't do anything foolish."

I got out of bed and went into the front room, one of the soldiers prodding me a bit with his bayonet. They weren't much taller than I was.

"Easy, boy," my father said.

He was in his pajamas. My mother was in her nightgown, her mouth open as if she couldn't believe what was happening. My father had his hands over his head. "Just do as they say. Come over here by us. Walk slow." His voice was calm, and I didn't think it sounded frightened.

But I thought my father might fight them, right there. I guess I expected him to do that. All my life he'd been telling me about guns and war. But suddenly it was different. And he did not fight.

One soldier held a rifle on us while the other searched the rooms. He came out of my room with Vulcan and a box of Remington shells. From the back porch, he brought my father's two shotguns and the rifle; also, the bullets and more shells. He took them out to the front porch.

The soldier guarding us used his left hand to pluck at his uniform. He said something in Japanese. My father shook his head. He didn't understand. Then the other soldier plucked at my pants and nodded toward my parents' bedroom.

"I think he wants us to put our clothes on," my father said. "You go in first, Cece."

The soldier nodded. He looked quite young and almost as nervous as we were.

When my mother came out, hands shaking badly, it was my turn. I put on a shirt, pants, boots and got my light parka. Then I joined them again, and my father got dressed, too.

We could hear voices out in the street. They'd gone house to house, awakening everyone. Now, they were gathering everyone out in the road. Soon the soldier nodded for us to leave, and we walked out ahead of him.

I whispered to my father, "Should we run?"

His answer was harsh. "No! They'll shoot."

We could see other people being marched toward the church. No one was saying anything. Everyone was still stunned.

Just as we got to the end of our walk, by the picket fence, Netsig came around the corner of the house. He hadn't been penned up in a long time and didn't stray far away. I guess he came out from the back yard because he sensed something was wrong.

I said, "Netsig, go back!"

But one of the soldiers raised his rifle.

Netsig kept coming, not meaning any harm. Yet I suppose he looked big and mean to the soldier. There was a shot, and I saw him topple over. I screamed, and immediately there were other shouts. No one knew who had been hit.

I started toward Netsig, sobbing, but the soldier in back of us shoved me against my father who grabbed my shoulder and said, "Don't!" He kept a grip on my arm as we went toward the church.

It felt like something was crushing my chest. Netsig

was dead! I hated that soldier. I also hated my father and Lieutenant McCall and all the sailors at Sedluk. They were cowards. They had let us be captured.

The soldiers ordered us inside and made us take seats. It was a long while before I stopped sobbing. Finally, I looked up and saw that everyone in Sedluk was there. Even old Bakutan had been routed off the high ridge and was also in the church. He was frowning.

I saw Char beside her parents and little brother. Then I saw Max in his summer pajamas and a light skin parka. Tony was down near the front. I could just see his head.

When they brought Mrs. Thorkilsen in, one of the soldiers gave her a rude half push toward the pews about midway down. She drew back a big hand as if to hit him. Some of the other soldiers laughed. One soldier pointed at her and shouted, "*Oki, oki.*" They all laughed. She sat down, glaring at him.

Then it got quiet, except for the little ones who were crying, and a Japanese officer came in. The soldiers jumped to attention as he strode down the aisle. In front of the church, he turned and faced us, scanning the audience.

Most of the soldiers had small noses, round faces, very slanted eyes and bad teeth, but this officer looked different. His nose was thinner and sharper, and his eyes were larger. His boots were shining, and he held a small black book in his hand.

He said, very slowly, "I am Major Eguchi, leader

of this occupation force. We are a unit of the Japanese Imperial Army." His English was good.

"I do not wish for anyone to be injured, so you will please listen and obey me. . . ."

"I . . ."

He paused to check the black book. I guess it was an English translation book. ". . . You are all prisoners of war, but you will be treated under the rules of the Geneva Convention. I have given orders to take all men over the age of sixteen to the island. We will arrange a prison out there until a ship arrives to take the American military personnel back to Japan."

A wave of shock swept the church. I looked at my father. He was staring at Major Eguchi, no expression on his face at all. My mother's eyes were closed, but I saw her reach for his hand.

Major Eguchi continued, "We do not wish to make prisoners of the families. The women and children may remain here in the village. But I have given orders for the guards to shoot anyone who attempts to leave." He paused and looked at our faces. "Do you understand?"

None of us answered.

"My soldiers have searched your houses for guns and ammunition, but if any of you have hidden guns you will tell us where they are. I will execute any person found with a weapon."

He let that sink in and then said something to one soldier, maybe a sergeant, standing near him. The soldier snapped his head in a bow.

The major spoke again, "All United States military

personnel will stand. All civilians over the age of sixteen will stand."

Lieutenant McCall, who had not spoken, got up slowly. "I am the commanding officer," he said.

Major Eguchi bowed slightly.

"I want a guarantee that your men will not harm the wives and children."

The major's dark eyes flickered. "I assure you that my men will not harm the civilians here unless they provoke harm."

Lieutenant McCall, his voice low and defeated, then said, "All right, we will do as he orders."

My father got up. The other men arose, too. But old Bakutan sat firmly in his pew. I don't think he really understood what was going on. A Japanese soldier nicked at him with his bayonet point. Baku roared in fury.

Major Eguchi saw what was happening and rattled off Japanese. The soldier pulled his bayonet away. The major said, "The old man can stay with the women and children."

I heard the lieutenant's voice again saying, "We'll fall in outside."

My father bent down to kiss my mother. She clung to him a moment. It was going on all over the church. Then he grabbed my hand. "Boy, do as the soldiers tell you."

For the first time in my life I saw tears in his eyes. My father and all the rest had been defeated without a shot being fired, aside from the bullet that had killed poor Netsig.

We watched in silence as they filed out of the church. None of the men looked back at us.

"In a day or two," Major Eguchi said, "I will issue regulations for this village, but I warn you again not to attempt to escape."

There was little chance of that, anyway. The next settlement was more than a hundred miles away, through wilderness. On foot, it would takes weeks to reach Nome and the few Army troops there.

The major went on, "There will be guards stationed in the village, and anyone causing trouble will be taken to the island. No one will be permitted outside after six o'clock in the evening. You may leave your homes for anything that is necessary after six o'clock in the morning. Food will be rationed, but I will cover that in the regulations."

Behind us, a mother said, "Where did he learn to speak English like that?"

The major overheard. He answered steadily, "I attended Stanford University for four years."

Mrs. Thorkilsen piped up, "This is a nice way to show your gratitude."

The major ignored her. "You may go to your homes now."

Miss Etheridge stood up meekly. "Sir, we have two weeks of school left. I would like the children to finish this term."

Major Eguchi was abrupt. "No! There will be no public gatherings."

She sat down, but Mrs. Thorkilsen spoke up again. "You Nips are against education, too!"

The major stared angrily at her, then spoke to the soldiers in Japanese. They waved their rifles toward the door, and we filed out.

Netsig was still in the yard where he had fallen. I couldn't look at him, but my mother said, "We must bury him, Dory. We'll do it together."

[2]

Later that same day, Major Eguchi sent word to Miss Etheridge that he had changed his mind and would let school continue. I'm sure Mrs. Thorkilsen's remarks had provoked him. I remember that Miss Etheridge went from house to house to spread the word.

When she came to ours, she said, "Dory, would you take on the job of opening the school in the morning?" In the past, one of the enlisted men from the cannery detail had always come up to light the oil stove and raise the flag. We usually took turns ringing the bell.

I said I would, but when she was leaving I couldn't resist saying, "Now, you see what's happened! My father's a prisoner on Unigak. Do you like that?"

"Dory!" my mother said sharply.

Miss Etheridge answered, "It's all right, Mrs. Scofield. Dory and I don't agree about war." Then she went next door.

It was awful looking out at the island and knowing the Japanese had my father. Everywhere in our house there were signs of him: his fishing rods on the back porch; his picture in dress whites just after he made chief petty officer, on the radio cabinet.

My mother said, "We have to stay busy and try not to think of him out there."

"Won't help come?" I asked.

My mother nodded. "I'm sure it will. Meanwhile, we'll help your father and the other men. We'll mind our business."

"Will they send ships and planes here?"

"I don't know, Dory."

"Will they have to bombard the island before they send troops ashore to get the Japanese?" I asked.

My mother got irritated. I guess she didn't want to think about that. She said, "Find something to do with yourself."

I went out into the road and sat by the edge, hoping that Char or Max or Tony would see me. There were two guards on patrol, and they walked up and down the road, starting at the cannery and going all the way up to the school and back. They had brown cloth strips wrapped around their legs.

I held my head down when one of them passed. I couldn't get over how small they were. Once, one lifted his helmet to wipe sweat from his forehead. He looked like a high school boy.

Finally, Tony came out on his porch and saw me. I waved and he came over, squatting down beside me. Everything seemed so gloomy and bad it was hard to talk about it. "We've got to go somewhere for help," I said.

"Kwiguk. There are some men there," he said.

I think we both knew it was useless. What could a few men at Kwiguk or Alakanuk do to help us? The Japanese would either shoot them down or take them prisoner.

We changed the subject. I said, "Tony, I swear I'm going to kill the soldier that shot Netsig. I'll know him when I see him."

Tony said, "Yeh."

It was big talk. My stomach got knotty when I saw one of them.

"Maybe Bakutan could sneak away for help," I said.

Tony answered, "Yeh."

It was a difficult day. All we could do was talk and watch the guards go back and forth, back and forth.

The next morning I went up to the school about seven o'clock, lit the oil stove to take the chill off, emptied the wastebaskets and then went home for breakfast. A few minutes before eight I went back to raise the flag. Then school started.

Miss Etheridge was very nervous. We weren't accomplishing much, but she was trying. Things were settling down about ten o'clock when there was a knock at the door. Tony and I got up to open it. Major Eguchi was standing at the bottom step. A guard was with him.

Miss Etheridge came out.

The major said curtly, "This is Japanese-occupied territory. You will take the American flag down and replace it with the Imperial flag." He took the Japanese flag the guard was holding.

Miss Etheridge nodded. She said, "Tony, please do it." He was nearest the major.

I couldn't believe it. She didn't argue or stand up to him at all.

Thinking about our fathers on Unigak, I said, "Tony, don't!"

Miss Etheridge gasped.

The major laughed, glanced at me, and said, "Maybe you'd like to go to the island, too? How old are you?"

"I'm thirteen," I answered, finding courage from somewhere to meet his eyes.

He grunted and then looked back at Miss Etheridge. He barked something at the guard, who gave a quick bow with his head and ran to the flagpole. The American flag came down, and the Japanese flag went up. I felt sick.

The major went past us and into the school. We watched from the door. He went up to the front and jerked the American flag from its staff. As he passed Miss Etheridge again, he said, "No American flags will be displayed in this village."

She didn't answer, and he returned toward the floating dock.

In a few days the major finally issued his regulations. There was a long list of things we could and couldn't do. The third day they searched our houses again for weapons but didn't find any. The regulations had four or five paragraphs, as I remember, on guns and attempting to escape.

Mrs. Thorkilsen caused a fuss one night when she went out of her house after six o'clock. The youngest DiSantis boy had bronchitis, and she'd been treating him now that Pharmacist Mate Robbins was on Unigak. A guard stopped her, and before it was settled Major Eguchi had to come over from the island.

I think Mrs. Thorkilsen and my mother helped hold the settlement together during the first ten days of the occupation. Some of the mothers wouldn't even leave the houses, and I noticed that Max Unger was awfully scarce on the road in the afternoons. Aside from school, he stayed inside.

I remember my mother sticking a big pair of shears into her pocketbook the first time she went out to draw our weekly rations at the cannery. The Japanese were giving us two pounds of flour, a half pound of sugar and a half pound of coffee each week.

I watched from our window when a guard stopped her to look into the pocketbook as if she might be hiding a pistol. I always thought my mother was a very gentle person, but when the guard took the scissors, she snatched them right back. When she returned to the house, she had to sit down to settle her nerves.

Later, she said, "Don't be uppity with them but don't be afraid of them either. Your father and I were raised in the country, and we just never got afraid of flesh and blood folks. That's what they are, Japs or not."

[3]

The official Army history says that five flights were made over Unigak to scout the enemy's defenses during the first ten days of occupation, but we only saw one aircraft. A Navy patrol plane broke out of the cloud cover over the island one afternoon but ducked back in when the Japanese began firing. We could see black puffs of smoke in the sky and heard the dull bangs of the anti-aircraft guns.

We were beginning to know what war was really like, and we felt helpless, locked up in the settlement across from Unigak.

Then on the fourteenth night, Yala, one of the Eskimo women, said she heard an aircraft drone to the east of us, out over the plain. She had very sharp ears. No one else heard it, but the dogs did bark for a long time that night.

We could feel something was happening, but didn't know what until early in the afternoon of the sixteenth day when the front door of the school, squeaking as usual, opened slowly. We heard the squeak and saw a man step inside. He closed the door and stood with his back against it. His dark eyes swept over everything. He held a rifle.

He was dressed like a hunter and, in some ways, resembled an Eskimo. Or perhaps an Indian. His skin had a deep copper tone, and the sweat on his face made it shine along broad cheek bones. He was not too tall but appeared lean and muscular.

Something else we immediately noticed—mud on his boots and on his blue corduroy pants and light skin parka. Likely, he had come down off the plain.

The parka was partially open and revealed a heavy pistol—it looked like a .45—strapped to a web belt on his side. I knew that no hunters around our area owned a pistol like that. This man had come from far away.

I think that if a pencil had dropped it might have sounded like a tree crashing. It was that silent as he stood there, one hand still on the doorknob.

"Are there any Japanese guards in the settlement?" he asked.

Miss Etheridge managed to find her voice. "There are usually six guards here."

That was wrong. There were six guards, but only two at a time in the village.

"Where?" he asked, sounding almost angry.

Later, I realized he was just very tense. I looked away from him and back at her. She was behind the desk. Her face was pale, and I saw that her hands were shaking. Our Miss Partridge wasn't up to situations like this. Mrs. Thorkilsen would already have made him state his business.

She answered, "They have regular patrols," and then put her hands down on the desk, holding on trying to anchor that small body. Her iceberg-blue eyes were wide and staring.

"Where did they take the military personnel?"

"To the island, across there," she said, pointing.

He walked quickly to one of the five large windows that faced south toward the settlement, glancing down the road toward the houses. Then he drew back. The fog was patchy, and he couldn't see very much.

By this time, all of us were nervous, especially the little ones. I strained my eyes to see if the safety catch on his rifle was engaged. It wasn't. He could shoot at any second.

He moved from the south wall and the windows to walk through the middle of the room, threading the desks until he was standing only a few feet from Miss Etheridge.

Weakly, she asked, "Who are you?"

He looked at the class again, seeming to study each face. Why, I still don't know. Perhaps he was making sure that there were no Japanese in the room. Then he said to her, "May I speak to you in private?"

Under any other circumstance, the whole room would have laughed. There were no private places in the Sedluk school, except the broom and storage closet and the bathrooms.

I saw Miss Etheridge trying to gather her wits. Finally, she said, "Children, we didn't have a song session Tuesday, so let's make up for it this afternoon."

She blew her pipe and started us off in "Alouette." At the time, I thought it was silly, but it did give them a chance to talk.

She stepped up near the blackboard with him. We were watching closely, and most of us didn't sing very well or very loud. We were trying to listen to what he was saying. Only the little ones, in the front, were singing loud.

When "Alouette" ended, Miss Etheridge came back to her desk to face us. She did not seem frightened any longer. Her hands weren't shaking. We were all puzzled, wondering what he'd told her, wondering who he was.

She smiled a little when she said, "We'll change the schedule now. I'd like you to go out into the schoolyard and take another recreation period. Please do not look back at the building. Play just as you did this morning." She paused, glancing at the muddy stranger again. "One more thing, if any of you see the Japanese guards headed this way, shout my name as loud as you can. But keep playing! All right?"

As Max Unger passed me, he muttered, "You see that pistol?" At a time like this, all sorts of crazy things come into your mind: He'd killed someone at Goodnews or Platinum, then made his way along the coast or over the mountains. Half-breed, crazy, dangerous Eskimo and Miss Etheridge didn't realize it.

Just as I was going through the door, ready to talk to Tony or Max about running to the settlement and warning the mothers, Miss Etheridge called out, "Dory, could you stay please?"

When the others had gone, Miss Etheridge said to him, "Dory is our most experienced boy when it comes to the countryside here. I think he can help you, Lieutenant."

Lieutenant. I wondered about that as she went on,

"Dory is the son of Chief Radioman Scofield, one of the men being held on Unigak."

I shook his hand.

Brown eyes digging into mine, he asked, "Can I trust you, Dory? It could mean your life, even your father's life."

That only made me more jumpy than ever.

Miss Etheridge smiled encouragement. She said, "Dory is very trustworthy."

He was thoughtful a moment, perhaps thinking how much to tell me, and then leaned back against the desk, propping the rifle beside it, his hand lingering on it. The safety was still off. He didn't take his eyes off me while he talked.

"I'm with a special unit of the Army. I was dropped here by parachute two nights ago to scout the defenses on Unigak. . . ."

Yala had been right! She *had* heard an aircraft drone over the plain.

". . . There were two of us, dropped about ten miles from here, inland, with some equipment. But the other officer is dead. . . ."

Now that he was a little more relaxed, we could see how very tired he was. His eyes were bloodshot, and the skin beneath them was puffy. His hands shook slightly, I noticed, but I'm sure that was because he was so tired.

"His chute didn't open all the way, and he was badly injured on impact. He died early last night. I buried him this morning and came on here. The first building I saw was the school. . . ."

I began to realize that the lieutenant was not as old as I had first thought. In his late twenties, probably. Only fifteen or sixteen years older than I was. I began to be less nervous about him.

"Now, the important part," he said. "I have to report on the number of Japanese soldiers on Unigak and the guns they have for defense. We tried to scout it by air last week, but the cloud cover was too heavy."

Miss Etheridge spoke up. "You see, Dory, the lieutenant needs a guide to get him to Unigak, someone who knows every inch of the island, someone who can take him there tonight."

I heard myself volunteering, "I know the island."

I also knew there were several kayaks up on racks in Porter's Cove, about three miles north of the settlement. I was sure the Japanese hadn't found them because the cove was hidden. Last time I had been there, in May, there was also as old umiak, a medium-sized skin boat, perched up behind the kayaks. We could use it if the lieutenant couldn't handle a kayak.

The lieutenant hesitated. "I wasn't really thinking of you."

In a way, I guess I was relieved. But I was disappointed, too. I was sure I could lead the lieutenant to Unigak and then ashore. Crossing the strait this time of year wasn't difficult. There was no ice, and the sea was usually smooth under the patchy fog.

"Bakutan," I suggested.

He glanced at Miss Etheridge for approval. She nodded instantly. "Yes, he's the one."

"Can he be trusted?" the lieutenant asked.

She gave me a questioning look. I replied, "I think so." I was certain he could be trusted. I knew he was angry because the Japanese had taken his guns.

"You really don't have too much choice, Lieutenant," Miss Etheridge said. "He's the only man left in the settlement."

We talked a few minutes longer, and then Miss Etheridge volunteered to speak to Bakutan, but the lieutenant didn't like that idea. Being a woman and not knowing the ridge, she'd have to take the path to reach his hut. Likely, she'd be seen.

The lieutenant turned to me. "Can you do it? Can you slip up there without anyone seeing you?"

"I can go along the back of the ridge," I answered, my heart drumming.

I remember that Miss Etheridge protested. She broke in, "I don't like this. The children shouldn't be involved."

The lieutenant seemed to ignore her. He nodded at me. "Okay, contact him and ask him to come here at eight o'clock if this fog holds. Tell him not to let anyone know he's coming. Is he up there alone?"

"Just some dogs."

The lieutenant nodded again. "I guess that's about it. But be careful. I'd do this myself except I don't know the area. I might be caught."

Chances were very good he'd be caught.

Miss Etheridge had been looking at him as if she couldn't quite believe this was happening. Neither could I, really. It meant, I thought, that our fathers would soon be rescued from the island.

I heard Miss Etheridge asking him for his name.

He looked at her for a moment and then answered, "Harry Forbes."

Somehow, the way he said it, we both knew that it wasn't his real name.

There were so many questions I wanted to ask him, but I didn't dare to. I'd read about men like Harry Forbes. The British and French had them operating behind enemy lines. They parachuted in to do what he was doing right now. They spied on the enemy, blew up bridges and sent messages back to London. I was certain he was that kind of soldier.

I did ask one question. "Are you Eskimo?"

He laughed softly. "No, half Indian. Blackfoot tribe."

My guess hadn't been far off.

He studied me. "If you're caught this afternoon, it will be healthier for you to say you've never seen this Indian in your life." Then he turned to Miss Etheridge. "Is there any place I can grab a few hours' sleep until that old man can get down here?"

Miss Etheridge glanced at me and then said, "You can't stay here, Lieutenant. You'll endanger us."

"You like the idea of the Japanese being here?"

Her face flushed. "The broom closet, that's all we have," she finally answered, tipping her head toward it. "Are you hungry?"

The lieutenant shook his head and again went to the windows on the south side. Satisfying himself that no guards were near, he disappeared into the small space and closed the door.

Miss Etheridge looked at the closet for a moment and then murmured, "I don't know. I just don't know. He shouldn't have come here to the school. He should have hidden on the plain."

"He had to come here to get a guide," I said. She didn't answer.

I was excited now and couldn't wait to tell my mother. "This means the Army will land here and recapture Unigak."

Frowning, she said, "I suppose so."

We went outside but Miss Etheridge paused on the stoop to look off toward the settlement. All day, the fog had been thick over the bay and strait; sometimes rolling in to blanket Sedluk back to the ridge; then pulling out again. There were still drifting patches of it, crossing the road now and then, blotting out the cannery and church. It was safe for her to talk.

The children stopped playing as soon as they saw us. Miss Etheridge walked over to them. I followed, but before she could say a word, Max, Tony and Char came rushing up. Tony asked breathlessly, "Who is he?"

I didn't answer because Miss Etheridge was already starting to speak. She told them that he was an American soldier, that he was here to help Sedluk, and that she would get word to the mothers. "But you must promise me not to say anything about him."

Heads turned to look at the school building. Max asked, in a whisper, "What is he?"

"A commando," I said. Tony's mouth dropped.

Miss Etheridge took a few more minutes to talk to the little ones. She was concerned about them blabbing. She started calling each by name, asking them to make a solemn promise not to talk about the stranger.

Then, scanning the road again, she said, "Now, we'll go back inside just as if nothing had happened." She checked her watch. "We still have another hour of school."

If the temperature had turned tropical, she would have kept school anyway. She let us out at three. I guess the lieutenant was sound asleep.

[4]

I blurted it all out.

At first, my mother didn't believe me. Then she took off her apron and sat down in the front room, shaking her head. She was excited by the news. But I suppose she was worried, too.

She said, "Why couldn't this lieutenant do it himself? He's a grown man and a soldier."

I explained why. "Besides, I don't think Baku would even talk to him."

She said, "Maybe I should go."

"You'd have to take the path. I can climb the ridge. They won't see me."

"I think I'll make some fresh coffee," she said. She never drank coffee after the breakfast hour. Going into the kitchen, she paused at the door. "I expect your father would want you to do this. I don't know." She sighed and went on in.

The time from just after three dragged on slowly. I wandered about the house, now and then looking out at Unigak. I couldn't wait for night to go to Bakutan's, simply because there was no night. So I decided to go at five-thirty, when the garrison on Unigak sent the evening food boat to the guards in Sedluk.

About five-thirty, when I went out into the front room I saw the family Bible on the lamp table by my father's overstuffed chair and knew that my mother had been reading it. She always read it when there was trouble. Afterward, she'd seem very calm.

I watched by the front window until the prow of the food boat bumped up on the beach. I could see one guard down by the boat, getting the food; the other was probably on the road. It was time to go.

My mother pulled me close and held me a moment. Then she asked if I'd be warm enough, the exact way she'd asked it for years. This time it wasn't to go ice fishing or up on the plain to hunt wolverines. But the tone of her voice was the same. Then she said, "Silly me, it's summer, isn't it, Dory?"

I stood out in the back yard for a moment. It

was one of those rough times—like the moment before
your first dive off the high board while everyone is
watching. Or just before swinging across a railroad
trestle when you've been dared.

Our back door opened. My mother must have been
watching. She said, "Dory, it will be all right if you
don't go."

I began running straight toward the ridge line,
keeping hunched over. The going was wet and muddy.
I slipped and slid around. Finally, I crawled up the
sandstone slope and crossed over, then traveled along
the east side, going south toward Baku's, well back
from the high ridge so they wouldn't spot me. There
was no way of telling when the fog would hide me,
or when it wouldn't.

It was about six-fifteen when I got to Baku's place,
coming up from behind it. The dogs alerted him,
and he came out, holding a short fish spear in his
hands. When he recognized me, he lowered the spear.

"Baku, I need to talk to you. Can I come inside?"

He made a grunting noise and turned to re-enter
the small outer room where his gear was stored.
I followed him into the main room. It was smelly
and dark in there, as I expected. A little illumination
came through the intestine skylight. There was also
a yellow glow from his blubber lamp.

He was in the middle of his evening meal, and
he sat back down at the rough board table. He began
gumming a dried fish as he waited for me to speak.
Beside his plate was a bowl of some kind of gravy.

I took a deep breath—I had run most of the way—

and said, "Baku, a man from the Army needs your help."

He didn't even pause from taking a chunk of bannock and sopping up gravy to stuff into his toothless mouth. I wasn't sure he had understood me so I repeated it, adding, "He needs a guide to take him to Unigak tonight."

Baku finally looked up, staring at me. His face was bronze in the yellow light. He mumbled, "No Unigak." With that, he tore off another piece of the griddlecake and dipped it into the bowl. "Japanese on Unigak. No Unigak."

I said urgently, "Baku, this man is here to help us get the Japanese off Unigak."

He repeated, "No Unigak." He was the most stubborn man that ever lived.

Desperate now, I went up to the table and said, "Baku, your friend Nante is out there. If you help this man, he will be released."

Baku glanced up. "Nante?" he asked.

"Yes."

He looked down again. "Nante is okay," he said. "He is Eskimo."

I felt helpless and wondered how to make him understand. I said, "Nante will be free! Anat and the other Eskimos will be free if you help. My father will be free."

He grunted something I couldn't understand and then reached over to stab another piece of fish with his sharp knife.

"Baku," I said—maybe angrily—"you must do this for the government, for everyone in Sedluk."

He pretended not to hear.

"Are you listening?" I shouted.

He looked up, his ancient eyes like frozen nubs of black iron. "No Unigak."

I knew then that he would say nothing else, and I also knew that he would not guide the lieutenant. I must have stood there for two or three minutes, unable to believe that anyone could be so mean.

I couldn't understand old Baku. We had been friends. He knew almost every rock on Unigak. I don't think he was too frightened of the Japanese. I could only guess that he was just very set in his ways. An old, stubborn man who didn't care about anyone.

"Coward, coward," I screamed at him.

He didn't even look up.

I fled from his hut, tears in my eyes. I was more angry than anything else. But I was hurt, too. I thought he'd do it for me if no one else.

Returning along the ridge top, I suddenly realized that I would have to take the lieutenant to Unigak. None of the mothers knew much about the island. I thought of Mrs. Thorkilsen, but she was almost sixty. So far as I knew, Miss Etheridge had been there only twice. With the exception of Mrs. Thorkilsen, none of the women had ever paddled a umiak. Stopping once to rest, I broke out in a sweat just thinking about going over to the island.

As I crossed the tundra, after coming down off the

ridge, I had another thought. I decided to ask Char Midgett to go, too. Both Tony and Max were clumsy when they paddled a boat. They made a lot of noise. Char could paddle almost silently. We'd do better with three paddlers.

I got home about seven-fifteen, and my mother was waiting by the back door. I don't think she'd left it. She said, "My heart's been in my mouth for almost two hours." She looked at me, made a funny noise in her throat, and complained, in a joking way, about the mud on my boots.

Of course, she asked about Baku. I said everything was all right; that he'd take the lieutenant across. I couldn't tell her, just yet, what the old man had really done.

She let out a sigh of relief and said, "Now, we'll just stay safe and snug in this house until it's all over." She went to the stove to warm up corn bread and salmon patties.

I went out to the front window. The wall of fog had pushed in solidly again. Sedluk was blanketed. Unigak was completely socked in. If it held, we could cross straight over. If it began to get patchy or lifted, we could go north a bit and come down on the island that way.

I slipped out of the house, went around the side, and then crossed the back yards until I got to Char's. Her kid sister answered the door, and in a moment Char came out. I got her to follow me to the edge of her back yard so we could talk. Then I told her about Baku and what had to be done.

"All we have to do is paddle and then get him up near the station."

She tugged at the collar of her woolen shirt and chewed on her lip. She didn't want to go. But finally, she nodded. She was worth more than Tony, Max and Baku put together.

"You'll have to sneak out of the house and not let your mother know."

She nodded again.

"I'll be back in about a half hour," I said.

Char started to say something but then turned and ran into her house. I went back home and got into the front room just as my mother was calling out to say that dinner was ready.

It was hard to get anything down.

[5]

Char heard me coming and whispered, "Dory, I'm here."

She was standing at the corner of her house, bundled in a light parka; the soft, dark hair tucked up inside a blue stocking cap. I started to say something, but she held a finger to her lips, pointing to her bedroom window. It was still open where she'd crawled out.

We cut between the houses and the tundra edge, staying off the road to circle up behind the school and come down on it from the inland side. The visibility wasn't more than fifty feet.

About a hundred yards from the building we stopped, listening for any sounds. It was quiet, and no one was following us, so we edged around the building to the stoop. I knocked very gently. As quietly as I could, I said, "It's me, Dory Scofield."

He must have heard us coming because he was poised behind the door. It squeaked as he opened it, and he made a face. He looked down at us and asked, "Where's the old man?"

"He wouldn't do it, Lieutenant," I said.

"Wouldn't do it?" I think he was shocked.

"No, sir."

He told us to come inside.

"Can anyone else talk to him, one of the mothers?" he asked.

"He won't do it." I was certain of that.

His face stormed up, and he cursed softly. Then he said, "All right, go on back home. Thanks for trying."

I said, "We're going to take you. We know the way."

He laughed. "Run along now. I appreciate what you've done. I'll find a way to get over there."

"You can't, Lieutenant, not unless you know where Porter's Cove is. You can't do it then unless you know how to paddle a kayak. They tip easy. But there's a umiak there, a skin boat. It'll take all of us. And it's not too big to handle."

He was frowning and peered closer at Char. "Is that a girl?" I guess he saw her hair.

I told him it was Char Midgett.

"I'll be damned," he said.

I said, "We can help you paddle across and then lead you to the station. We'll hide and wait for you. We've been over there dozens of times."

He shook his head. "I'm not about to get two kids shot up. I don't know what I'll run into over there. Now, thanks again, but go on home."

I insisted, "Lieutenant, you'll never get there. The Japanese took all the boats and kayaks except the ones in Porter's Cove. There's a rowboat down by the floating dock but it's chained."

He stood there frowning at us in the shadowy light. Finally, he said to Char, "You think you can do it?"

Her voice was no more than a high croak when she answered him. Mine hadn't been much better.

The lieutenant laughed weakly. "I've got to be insane but okay. You do exactly as I say. You understand? No heroics."

We nodded.

"Which way do we go?" he asked.

"North."

So we headed out for Porter's Cove, named after a trapper long dead. Just before we left the road to take the trail that ran along the cliff edge, the lieutenant stopped to scoop up a handful of mud. He smeared it over his face and hands. He looked at us and said, "You need it more than I do."

We didn't ask why, but he explained anyway. "If that fog suddenly lifts, we'll make pretty good targets. You both have very white skins."

Char and I looked at each other. I don't think we had really realized what we were doing until that moment. We would have been happy to turn back.

We got to Porter's about nine o'clock. It was the best protected cove along our section of the bay. That's why the kayak and umiak frames were kept there during the winter. In readiness for summer, the skins had been laced back on them just a week or so before the Japanese had arrived. They were on racks about four feet off the ground.

We lifted the umiak down. It wasn't very heavy. It was one of the smaller ones, about twenty or twenty-one feet long. In Greenland, they are called *women's* boats. Two or three people can handle them easily.

The lieutenant took the bow while Char and I carried the stern. He put his rifle in and took a small pocket compass from his pocket. Then we shoved off into the thick murk. It was still light, of course, since the short period of twilight wouldn't come for another three hours. We were encased in wet grayness.

There was no wind. The surface of the bay was smooth, almost oily. The current drifted to the north, but if we kept a few points to the southwest, as my father always did, we'd go straight to Unigak. Holding the rifle in his lap, the lieutenant sat in the bow, paddling expertly, now and then checking his compass. We didn't talk at all. Not even a whisper.

Occasionally, a duck would flutter up from the water ahead of us, batting its wings in a dripping take-off, and we'd all freeze. You could hear three breaths suck in simultaneously. I think it even got to the lieutenant's trigger finger. The rifle would level. But we slid across the strait without any trouble and reached Unigak about ten o'clock.

North Point came up out of the fog, jagged and rocky. It was always dangerous because of the shelf that extended out from it, three or four inches below the water at high tide. It could easily rip the hull of a skin boat. So I motioned to the lieutenant, and we turned south, staying offshore about fifty feet, creeping along. There was a sandy beach about a mile below North Point, a good landing beach.

Once, Char turned to look back at me. Her face was tense, but she smiled. Or half smiled. She hadn't made one paddle noise all the way across. I'd made quite a few. Her muddy face looked funny.

If you look on the maps, Unigak Island is shaped like a banana leaf, with the small end at the north. The Foot is near the big end at the south. Tundra covers it between slabs of flat rock, and until the Navy took it over to build the radio station, only birds and seals inhabited it.

It took us another half hour to find the beach. When we nosed into shore, the lieutenant was very nervous. I guess he was half expecting to find a Japanese patrol there. He had his rifle up. He jumped out, made a quick reconnaissance of the beach and then returned. We pulled the umiak up and rested for a moment.

We felt pretty good when he told us that he'd rather have us than a half-dozen soldiers. He said soldiers would have been knocking the paddles against the side of the boat.

We led the umiak along the water's edge about two hundred feet north and hid it as best we could. At least, it wouldn't be very evident in the fog if a patrol did stop by the beach.

In the distance, we could hear the sing-song echo of Japanese voices and faintly, now and then, the whining and plunking of oriental music. It sounded like a windup record player. Once, coarse laughter drifted to us through the fog.

I don't know about Char's throat but mine was very dry. My stomach felt hollow.

The lieutenant, hearing the laughter drifting toward us, got close to our ears. He said, "If you're scared, join the club. So am I." That made us feel a little better.

He got us over behind some big rocks, took a map out of his parka and shined a tiny beam of light on it. I could see that it was a chart of Unigak, with the location of the station buildings marked on it. He asked quietly, "Where are the trails?"

There was a crooked trail that led up from the small beach that we were on. It went to the station. "Okay, I'll stay away from that one. Where are the others?" I showed him the one that led to The Foot. There were also a couple that went north to south.

"What's the best way to get to that west beach?"

he asked. "If they have any heavy guns, that's where they'll be."

"Go across the rocks around this end," I said. "There's a trail there, too."

"I'll stay off it," he murmured and then flicked the light off. He whispered, "You guys stay here. Don't move around. If any Japanese stray down here and find you, just hold your hands up and play dumb. If you hear any shots, get into that boat and paddle like hell. Otherwise, I'll be back in an hour or so."

He stood up, gave us a pat on the shoulder, reached into his parka pocket for a cold cigar stub, stuck it into his mouth and then vanished into the fog.

Huddled down there in the rocks, we began the long wait. It was damp and chilly, and water droplets had formed on Char's hair and on her stocking cap. We listened so hard that our ears almost hurt.

The sounds from the station were muffled but did not change. We could see white glows on the mist bank over there; red glows high in the air on the towers. From the Sedluk side, we could hear a dog bark now and then. But it was very quiet from that side. The 6 p.m. curfew made it like a ghost town.

The only way we could talk was almost mouth to ear, so we were sprawled out against each other. Char said, "My mother knows I'm gone by now. She'll be worried."

"Mine will, too. But it'll be okay after we explain."

"I hope so," Char said.

I was really thinking more about my father than my

mother, wishing he knew that I was on the island; that soon they'd all be free.

Char was silent awhile and then said, "If something bad happens to us, Dory, I hope it happens to both of us."

I asked her what she meant.

"If the Japanese find us," she said. "If they shoot."

It was what my father might have called "female thinking," but I looked at her muddy face and understood, maybe for the first time, what girls like Char were all about. She took my hand and held it tightly. Sometimes, she seemed a lot older than she was.

For the next half hour we talked about some pretty crazy things, backward and forward—back before we knew each other, and forward to what we might be doing when we left Sedluk, which wouldn't be any later than September. My father had gotten his orders for the *Yorktown,* and her father had applied for sea duty, too. We talked to shut out the Japanese sounds from the station.

It must have been about a quarter to eleven when we heard voices coming toward us, the sounds muffled by the fog. Then we could hear the scrape of feet. Char looked at me, and for a moment I thought she might cry. Her lips were pressed together. Whoever they were, they were coming down the crooked trail that led to the beach.

A moment later, we knew they were Japanese. We could hear the low sing-song. Once, we heard a guttural laugh.

Carefully, we moved back deeper into the rocks, knowing that if they saw the umiak they would begin a search.

One of them was carrying a flashlight, and the beam bobbed up and down in the murk. Then they stopped, probably just at the head of the beach. We didn't dare look.

One of them said something, and I guess the other one threw a rock into the water. A duck took off. We could hear his wings whirring. They both laughed.

We huddled together, eyes closed. Char kept pressing my hand.

Feet began to move again, and the sing-song voices retreated in the fog back up the crooked trail. After a long time I whispered to Char, "I feel like I don't have any bones in my legs." She laughed weakly.

That night on the shore of Unigak, I was probably as much in love with Char Midgett as I'll ever be with anyone.

About eleven-thirty, we heard footsteps again. We hugged the damp tundra behind the rocks and stayed very still, hardly breathing, hoping that this time it was the lieutenant. There had been no shots, and the station noises had quieted down.

We heard his voice in a hoarse whisper. "It's okay, it's me."

He came over and knelt down beside us. He was sweaty, and there was a worried look on his face. He whispered, "Let's get out of here. Quickly."

We lost no time in launching the umiak and paddling it back toward Porter's Cove.

[6]

At the school, the lieutenant asked, "Are you beat? I could use some help for another hour or so."

I was tired, but now that the Unigak thing was over I felt I could go all night.

He said, "I've got to make a radio call and shift some equipment farther inland. I brought it too close to the ridge."

Char wanted to go, too, but the lieutenant said no. He told her he didn't know how to thank her but that she should go on home to her mother. I told her to tell mine that I was okay and would be home in an hour or so. She went off into the fog toward the houses. It was about 1 A.M.

In back of the school, he checked the small compass. Then we started off. I had no idea where we were going and didn't ask. He moved steadily east across the tundra, now and then glancing at the compass. I had trouble keeping up with him because his legs covered so much ground. But the only time he looked back was when I fell. Even then, he said nothing; just waited until I got on my feet again. In some ways, he reminded me of my father.

We climbed the ridge just as twilight ended, leaving the fog below and behind us. He checked the compass again, and we angled northeast, following a set of footprints. I made a guess they were his.

Finally, about a mile and a half in, he stopped and

took another bearing, then walked a short distance to some large rocks.

Tucked in tight under an overhang were two packages wrapped in greasy black cloth, a square package wrapped in olive-colored canvas and a knapsack. One of the black cloth packages was long and narrow. It looked like it might hold guns. I was certain that the packages had been dropped by parachute with the lieutenant.

While he was pulling the olive canvas off the square box, he said, "I hid these here yesterday before I came to the school." The covering fell away, and I saw a portable radio set. It had Army Signal Corps markings on it.

He worked with it a minute or so, then spoke into the mike: "Morning Light, Morning Light, this is Asheville. This is Asheville! Come in. Over." There was no reply, and the lieutenant repeated the call.

Finally, there was a crackle from the receiver, and a voice answered, "Asheville, Asheville, I read you loud and clear. Go ahead."

The lieutenant spoke rapidly. "West beach okay for small craft landings. Gentle slope. No tide problems. Beach firm for tanks. Did you read me? Over."

Morning Light, whoever he was, answered, "Asheville, we read you."

Then another voice got on the air. "Is he dug in?"

"Morning Light, he's dug in with four heavy guns that look like 75 millimeters. He may have an infantry cannon. Six machine guns that look like 7 point 7 millimeters, air cooled. Estimated 350 to 500 troops.

It's a token force. His security isn't very good. I had no trouble. Over."

The "he," I knew, was the enemy.

Morning Light asked, "Can you blow the guns, Asheville? Over."

The lieutenant snapped, "Hell, no. I'm alone now. Holtz is dead. His chute . . ."

"Can you blow their ammunition dump as we come in? I'd like to take bearings on something in this fog."

The lieutenant swore under his breath and then barked back, "Morning Light, I told you I'm alone now."

The voice paid no attention, answering steadily, "Try it. We're holding to schedule despite the fog. Now, get off the air before he gets a fix on you. Good luck, Asheville."

The lieutenant seemed stunned. He stared at the radio set, then clicked it off. But suddenly, he shouted at it, "You're stark mad! You're asking me to fight a war with women and children. . . ."

I waited for him to cool down, then asked, "Who is Morning Light?"

He sighed. "He's a jackass."

Then the anger blazed again. "He's an Army colonel sitting on a Navy ship somewhere out there in the fog. He's the landing force commander, and he ought to have his head examined." The lieutenant's eyes looked as though they were on fire for a moment and then became weary again.

He wrapped the radio back into the canvas cover and nodded toward the oblong package at my feet.

"Can you carry that? I've got to move these farther away from the ridge."

I picked it up. It was very heavy, but I thought I could manage. When it got to my shoulder, I was positive it contained guns. I could feel two stocks side by side. The lieutenant lifted the radio set, and we started off, leaving the knapsack and the smaller square package. But then he decided to take the knapsack along.

We went about another mile inland and found some good rocks with overhangs. We hid the radio set and the package that I was carrying. Then we rested awhile, and the lieutenant opened the knapsack and took out some rations. He gave me two chunks of chocolate that were wrapped in silver foil.

"Lot of energy in that," he said.

We talked for a while.

The light was orange and it made his copper face look even darker. Most of the dried mud had peeled off because of sweat. He wouldn't say too much about himself, but I did find out that he'd been born in Montana and had gone to college on a football scholarship. From there, into the Army. He'd been an officer for two years and had taken jump training.

I was certain the Navy didn't have any Indians as commissioned officers. In fact, I wasn't even sure they had any Indian ratings, like chief or first class. The Indians were like the Negroes. The Navy didn't have any black men except for cooks and mess stewards. I told him that.

Looking off across the plain, he answered, "I guess

I lucked out." He was thoughtful a moment, then
added, "But they aren't particular any more. They got
a war to fight. All you have to do is breathe and walk
to get into it. I think you'll find war has a way of not
being choosy about anyone, white, black or red."

I remember saying, "I hear Indians are good
fighters."

He was amused at that. He laughed softly. "We
must not have been very good. You white people have
the country."

"If the history books are true, the white men had
all the guns. . . ."

"The books are right," he said. "On that point,
they're right."

"But they picked you to do this because you're a
good fighter, didn't they?"

His tired eyes were beginning to brood. "They
picked me because I looked like an Eskimo. Or an
Aleut. If I get caught, I might have a chance. Tell
them some phony story about wandering into Sedluk."

I didn't mean to upset him when I started, "But
Indians are . . ."

He got to his feet angrily. "Lay off that Indian
stuff, will you? That's practically the first thing you
asked me yesterday. I'm an officer in the United States
Army. Period!"

The lieutenant picked up his knapsack and rifle, and
we started back. After a quarter mile or so, he stopped
and apologized. He said, "After this mess is all over,
some day you can visit me in Montana, and I'll show

you what Indians are all about. Better still, I'll take you to Arizona. You'll learn something."

We went back to the first spot and he got the square black package, handling it very carefully. Later, I realized it was explosives of some sort.

At the low ridge line, we separated. I went home, and he went back to the school.

My mother was waiting up in the kitchen. She looked awful. As I came through the door, she said, "Thank God." She got up wearily and came over to me, holding me for a moment.

I started to explain, but she shushed me. "Char told me what happened. If you'd come in here two hours ago I would have swatted you. But I'm too worn out now. Never do that again."

Suddenly I was so tired I could hardly stand up. She said, "Get to bed, boy."

I took off my parka and boots and rolled in. She had a wash cloth and sat down on the edge of the bed to wipe my face. The last thing I heard, she was saying, "Never in my born days . . ."

Still very tired, I went to the school about seven forty-five. As I came through the door, Miss Etheridge was arguing with him. "You are not going to turn this school into an arsenal. The children are not going to fight this war. I want you out of here!"

I heard him answer calmly, "I'll be out of here tonight." He was still in the closet. The door was open.

I went by them to light the oil stove.

She turned to say, "Dory, you did go to Unigak with him last night. I can't believe it."

I nodded.

That made it worse. She turned back to him in a rage. "What right do you have to do this?"

He didn't even bother to answer her this time.

Her jaw was quivering as she looked at me. "Do you know what he has in there? Explosives!"

I nodded again but kept busy lighting the oilstove and adjusting the damper.

In all the months at Sedluk, I'd never seen our Miss Partridge so upset. Her face was red except around the lips. There was white anger all around them. She was glaring toward the closet. "You're endangering the lives of these children, of all of us."

His voice came out of the closet, low and cool. "That prairie isn't the safest place for me; think about it."

Miss Etheridge was speechless.

I walked over. He was sitting in there on a blanket —I suppose she'd brought it up the afternoon before when they were still friendly—working with a knife. He glanced up. "Good morning again," he said. A short, cold cigar was in his mouth. The knife was digging a small hole in something that looked like a cake of vanilla fudge. There was some fusing cord on the blanket. The lieutenant was making explosive charges.

"Absolutely not," Miss Etheridge said, "I want you out of this school!"

The lieutenant eyed her thoughtfully but didn't answer. I don't think he was trying to be stubborn. He was probably trying to figure out what to do.

Miss Etheridge mumbled something that neither of us understood and then ran out of the school.

Trying to explain her, I said, "She gets frightened easily."

He shifted the cigar butt in his lips, and I saw a trace of smile. "She's a good teacher, I'm sure," he said.

I decided to talk to Miss Etheridge and went outside. The fog had lifted a bit, and I looked across the road. She was down by the beach, staring at Unigak, barely visible across the way. I went down there.

Her eyes were red and puffy, but her voice was steady when she turned to say, "My first responsibility is to the school and the pupils. If the Japanese find out he's here, they'll fire at the school.

I told her what I'd heard out on the plain, about the Navy ships being in the outer bay, and about them asking him to go back to Unigak and blow the ammunition dump.

Her expression changed a bit, but she answered, "I'm certain they'll send him some help, Dory."

"It's too late for that."

I thought there was some guilt on her face when she turned to look back out at Unigak. I don't know. She did say, "I'm sorry he can't stay here." Then she walked back up to the school.

At eight-fifteen, I began pulling the rope on the *Edgerton* bell. School started as usual at eight-thirty.

Everyone looked at the closet door when they came in, knowing the lieutenant was in there. He had a flashlight and was still working away. I suppose Miss Etheridge had told him he could finish whatever he was doing.

But it was very tense in the room, and Miss Etheridge kept losing her thoughts. A few minutes after we'd pledged the flag, pointing toward the Stars and Stripes she had drawn on the board with colored chalk, Char dropped her Geography book. It hit with a splat. Miss Etheridge let out a little yelp, and I glanced at the closet door.

It was open a crack, and I could see the hole of a rifle barrel. Miss Etheridge noticed it, too, and clutched the top of her desk for support.

About ten minutes later, Tony happened to glance out of the south windows. He said excitedly, "The Japanese are coming."

We all got up to look. He was right. Major Eguchi and two guards were walking toward the school.

Miss Etheridge went quickly to the closet to whisper to the lieutenant. Back in front of the class again, her voice quivered as she said, "You must all act very naturally and don't look at the closet. Please don't."

She said to the primary students, "Now, take out your crayons and drawing paper. Use your imagination to draw me a beautiful tropical isle."

Then to the middle students she said, "You have your question and answer sheets on the Declaration of Independence. Please start them."

She looked at us in the back row. "Yesterday we

were studying the cultures of people as determined by climates. Today, I'd like you to prepare a list of architectural similarities in the warm climates around the world."

By the time Major Eguchi knocked at the door, we were all busy. But if Char had dropped her book again, the whole room would have exploded.

Miss Etheridge answered, in an almost normal voice, "Come in, please," and continued writing up reminders on the Declaration of Independence for the middles.

So far, the major had been polite to everyone in Sedluk. Firm, but polite.

"Good morning, Major," she said.

He answered back in Japanese, *"O-hai-yo."* Then added, very slowly, "You must learn to speak Japanese."

"It is a difficult language," Miss Etheridge replied.

Major Eguchi nodded and began walking toward the front of the class, looking down at what we were doing. All of us sat very still, but we heard Miss Etheridge say, "Children, please keep on with your lessons."

When he reached her desk, he said, "My guards report . . . that a student was seen returning to the village . . . last evening. . . ." He nodded toward the high ridge.

My throat got dry and my heart thudded, but for some reason he was looking at Max. Max just blinked.

Miss Etheridge cleared her throat. "I'm sure that your guards were mistaken. Perhaps it was old Baku-tan. He often moves back and forth along the ridge."

The major was looking around the room. Then he said, slowly and deliberately, "You must impress upon them that it is very dangerous to . . . leave the village. . . ."

"They know that, Major."

He turned and his eyes strayed to the blackboard. His voice became hard as he pointed to the flag drawn in red, white and blue. "Who did that?"

"I did," Miss Etheridge admitted.

"You will destroy it immediately. I gave strict orders that no American flags were to be seen in the village."

Miss Etheridge nodded. "Yes, Major." She stepped over to the blackboard to erase the flag.

He watched until it was a big colored smear, then began walking down the north side of the room, the broom closet side. He paused to sniff the air, a frown forming.

The cigar smoke, I thought.

Miss Etheridge called out sharply, "Major Eguchi!"

He turned.

She said, "I would like to ask your permission to take the children on a picnic this afternoon, outside the settlement."

He didn't answer right away, but stood there gazing at her, still trying to recognize the smell.

She continued, "They haven't been away from the settlement for two weeks now. It's very confining."

"What is a picnic?" he asked.

"Recreation."

"I see."

"I will take them just a short distance. Here, if you'll walk with me outside, I'll show you."

The major hesitated, then followed her as she passed him, going quickly by the broom closet. He didn't hear it, but there was a tremendous sigh of relief from everyone.

On the porch, I suppose she pointed off toward the coves that were dotted along the shoreline north of us. We heard her say, "One of the coves, not far in that direction."

The major spoke to one of the guards in Japanese. Then we heard him say, "A guard will go with you, Etheridge-san."

Before he left, he warned her again about movement outside the settlement and the flag. Then his boots clumped down the short flight of steps.

Miss Etheridge stayed out there a few minutes more, until the Japanese were well down the road. When she returned, her face was pale and strained, her hands shaking.

She opened the closet door, and we could see the lieutenant sitting in there. His face was pretty pasty, too. His rifle was in his hands. We knew that if Major Eguchi had opened the door, he would have fired.

All she said was, "Go now. I mean it."

He didn't need much urging. He got up and said, "Thanks for the use of the closet. Can I take the blanket with me?"

"Take anything you want," Miss Etheridge said.

He picked up his gear and the blanket and gave a slight wave to the class. Then he went on outside.

We stood up in our seats and watched as he went along the north side of the school and then started hurrying back across the tundra toward the high ridge and plain.

When we looked back at Miss Etheridge, she was standing by her desk, her head down. Finally, she lifted it to say, "Now, this is a school, and we have our lessons. . . ."

At about four that afternoon, a long time after the picnic was over, she came to our house carrying a book. Once she got into our front room, she asked where I thought the lieutenant might be. I told her where we'd hidden the weapons and radio set.

"I can take you up there easy," I said.

My mother broke in, "Dory, you're not leaving this house until all this is over. Miss Etheridge can find her way." Her voice was firm.

Miss Etheridge nodded.

I was certain she wanted to go up there and apologize to him; explain her feelings about war. Little good that would do him, I thought.

[7]

The next night, at about eleven o'clock, we were almost thrown from our beds when an explosion on Unigak sent shock waves toward Sedluk. My mother and I ran out to the front room to look seaward. The sky over the island was a dull red through the fog.

Above that, in the pale tan sky, was a twisting, expanding column of black smoke.

Then we heard the rumble of more explosions. They shook the house, rattling the windows and picture frames, banging the glasses together in the kitchen.

"The lieutenant blew the dump," I shouted. "The troops are landing."

My mother said, "Oh, yes, yes! Thank God."

Everyone poured out into the street to watch, wild with excitement. Then one of the mothers said, "The men could be injured," and everyone quieted down, just looking on.

The Japanese guards tried to herd us back into the houses, shouting angrily, but then they understood what was happening over on Unigak. They jabbered at each other and ran off toward the high ridge. No one chased them.

In a few more minutes, we could hear smaller guns firing. I knew they were rifles. Sometimes shouts echoed back across the strait. Twice, a ship's whistle sounded off. By midnight, the red glow had grown dimmer as if whatever was on fire had just about burned out. It was awful to stand there helplessly and not know what was going on.

I suddenly realized that Miss Etheridge was not out there with us. I was tempted to go up to her house. I said to my mother, "She's probably locked herself in. She's ashamed of herself."

"You let her alone," my mother ordered, looking back at the teacher's quarters. But I noticed that she was frowning, as if she was disappointed, too.

About twelve-thirty, it got very quiet. Even the dogs stopped barking. The mothers had begun to talk in low tones, and I think there was worry that the invasion had failed. My mother went home to get the binoculars, and with Tony and Char, I went to the dock. We thought we'd try to bust the rowboat lock, now that the guards had fled.

The phone rang in the cannery, and I think it was Mrs. DiSantis who went to answer it. A lot of people ran behind her. Those who didn't stood like statues, afraid that the voice on the other end might be the enemy.

It was Max Unger who raced out of the cannery, yelling, "We beat the Japanese! We beat the Japanese!"

For a moment, there was dead silence. Then you would have thought it was Christmas, the Fourth of July and everybody's birthday all at once. Tiny Sedluk came apart in shouts, tears and laughter.

The first whaleboat load arrived about one-thirty with some of the enlisted men, Chief Pharmacist Mate Robbins, Nante and an Army doctor. We all thronged to the floating dock to greet them. They yelled and shouted as the boat pulled alongside. Their faces seemed thinner, and they looked as though they needed a good bath, but no one was injured. My father wasn't aboard; neither was Lieutenant Forbes.

Chief Robbins sounded off, "Don't worry. They're fine. There'll be three more boatloads."

As they climbed out of the boat there was so much hugging and talking that it was hard to know what

was happening. The Army doctor started asking everyone onshore if he was needed. The men had been
concerned that we might need treatment.

My father arrived on the second boat, his face
gaunt and his eyes sunken a bit. He was pale, but he
was grinning and waving. As he jumped up on the
dock, he kissed my mother and held her. Then he said,
"Dory, Dory," and kissed me. It was the first time that
he had ever called me anything but "boy." And it was
the first time I could remember that he'd ever kissed
me.

He kept looking at us to see if we'd been hurt, and
we did the same to him. We walked together up to the
church, kind of holding each other. No one said to go
to the church, but it seemed the natural place for
everybody to be.

On the way there, my mother said, "That explosion
almost knocked us out of bed."

My father laughed weakly. "We were only a thousand yards away from it, but we didn't know what was
happening, either. They had us locked up in the machine shop, guards on every door and window."

When I could, I told him about Lieutenant Forbes. I
said he was the one who'd blown the dump and
described him.

My father shook his head. "Nope, I didn't see anyone like that. But there's a lot of confusion over there.
He probably joined up with the invasion commander."

Just at the entrance to the church, my mother said,
"Jake, it was Dory and Char Midgett who took the
lieutenant over to Unigak to scout. Night before last."

My father stopped and frowned down at me, then glanced at Mother with a puzzled look on his face.

"They took him across in a umiak so he could scout the Japanese. Your own son did that."

He stared at me and finally found his voice. "Why didn't you tell me?"

I heard my mother saying, "You taught him not to brag, Jake."

He lifted me off my feet in a hug. I felt very good.

The celebration lasted most of the night, although the little ones went back to bed about two-thirty. No one seemed to want to leave the church. Chief Robbins passed out all the medicinal brandy still left in sick bay. The adults sipped it and talked. Char and I got a lot of attention.

About three-thirty, when everyone was getting tired, the last boat arrived from Unigak, and the Army colonel who had commanded the landing forces came to the church with Lieutenant McCall. He brought a squad along to track down the guards. He was a short, stocky man and looked at us from behind steel-rimmed glasses. He seemed very calm and relaxed, cradling his helmet in folded arms. He said how proud he was to have led the troops ashore; that they had fought well. There was a lot of clapping.

When it died down, he went on, "We had casualties. They have to be expected in any war. So far as we know, there are nine United States personnel dead and twenty wounded. The enemy casualties are much higher." We all wondered about Major Eguchi, but no one asked.

My father stood up. "I'd like to find out about Lieutenant Forbes." He did it for my sake.

The colonel replied, "I haven't seen him as yet. He's probably very busy. We're still mopping up. He did a fine job of demolition."

There was applause again.

We went on home, tired but happy. Together again. At the front gate, my father and I lingered while my mother went up to Miss Etheridge's quarters and tapped on the door. There was no answer.

"Miss Etheridge must have gone for a long walk," she said when she returned.

"What's this all about?" my father asked, deep weariness showing in his face.

"I'll tell you later, Jake," my mother answered.

My head was so packed that it's a wonder I went to sleep. Just before I dozed off I kept hearing the things that had been said in church. *Why, Dory and Char took him over there. . . . Those kids ought to get a medal. . . .*

[8]

It was not until midmorning of the next day, when everyone was up and moving around again, that we learned there were actually eleven United States personnel dead. The lieutenant and Miss Sarah Etheridge had been added to the list. It was posted at the cannery.

Late that afternoon, my mother came into my room and put the blinds up. I'd been there all day.

There was no use telling myself, the big hero, that I had not meant saying those things to Miss Etheridge or thinking the things that I did.

Sitting on the edge of my bed, my mother said, "If you're the same as everybody else, you'll do this several times in your life. You'll want to take back every word and deed. It's painful, Dory. I know."

"I forced her to do it."

My mother shook her head. "She didn't go over there because of you, but for you."

If that was supposed to make me feel better, it didn't. It only chiseled into my head every unkind thing I'd said or thought about her.

The sergeant who had found the lieutenant and Miss Etheridge said they were close together, about a mile from the ammunition dump. They both had automatic weapons—probably the ones I'd carried—and each weapon had been fired. It was hard to imagine Miss Etheridge, who hated guns, who hated war, firing at the enemy.

Maybe she hadn't really shot either gun; maybe the lieutenant had fired them both while she reloaded. Yet I'm sure she didn't know how.

It was now certain that she had crossed over with him in the umiak in early evening. It was pulled up onshore on the same east beach that we'd used three nights before. But why had she decided to go with him? What had they talked about? Mother and I believe she'd gone up to the plain only to apologize; not to offer to help him. We'll never know what actually happened.

Char told me once that she thought Miss Etheridge had never shared an experience with a man and that this was her chance; that maybe they'd fallen in love out there on Sedluk plain. But that was like Char, hopelessly romantic.

The sergeant said it was probable that the lieutenant, after planting the charges, was spotted by a Japanese patrol. About two hundred feet away were five enemy casualties. They were in the line of fire from the lieutenant. And his body was blocking fire from Miss Etheridge.

The official Army history doesn't go into much detail. It simply states that "Miss Sarah Etheridge, a civilian teacher at Sedluk Settlement, volunteered to assist 1st. Lieutenant John Albert Coldwater [his real name] in planting demolition charges on an enemy-held installation during Operation Tundra. She lost her life in heroic support of Lieutenant Coldwater and has been awarded the nation's highest civilian medal. . . ."

Then there are several short paragraphs about Charlotte Midgett and Dory Scofield under the heading "Children Served, Too." They begin, "Dory Scofield and Charlotte Midgett, dependent children of naval personnel attached to the Naval Communications Station on Unigak Island, assisted in Operation Tundra. . . ."

About noon of June 26, a seaplane come in from Dutch Harbor. It had arrived to take Miss Etheridge and the lieutenant back to the States. A memorial service for them was scheduled for two o'clock down on the beach.

They were in two pine boxes that Nante had made. Flags were draped over each box, and a chaplain from one of the destroyer transports now anchored west of Unigak conducted the service.

The light was brown that day. The fog had moved out of the bay temporarily, and the sun was hazy behind high clouds. It was a quiet and pretty day, a peaceful day.

Mrs. Thorkilsen sang "Nearer My God to Thee," her dyed orange hair waving in the wind, and then the same honor guard that had greeted the new teacher the August before fired nine volleys over the pine boxes.

Char and I stayed close together, not looking at each other very much. Once I looked at my father. I knew that I would never again hear him howling a warrior's yell above the roar of an aircraft engine. He looked like a man with no insides.

A boat took the pine boxes out to the seaplane. They were placed aboard, and soon it began skimming across the strait. Then it lifted into the hazy sky. I was wishing I could tell Miss Etheridge before she left that I now agreed with her about guns and war.

We watched the plane until it was only a dot.

Everyone else began returning to their houses, but Char and I went on up the muddy road toward the school.

We stayed up there a long time, sitting on the stoop,

not saying much. Then Char asked, "Do you remember the first thing she wrote on the blackboard?"

I did. But I couldn't say it out loud, not just now. I couldn't form the words.

Char said, "Let's ring the bell."

So we went over and rang the *Edgerton* bell. It chimed clear and sweet off the ridges, back into the green valley and across the tawny plain to the low mountain foothills. It was not a sad sound. It was bright and joyous.

AUTHOR'S NOTE

The Children's War is purely a work of fiction, although the events it describes could have occurred in those bleak, jarring days of 1941–42. Japanese forces did invade and occupy Attu and Kiska, islands in the Aleutians; Dutch Harbor, the United States naval base on the island of Unalaska, was attacked. And the Navy did have remote listening posts to monitor broadcasts of potential enemies, although none existed near Norton Sound. The settlement of Sedluk and the island of Unigak are both imaginary, as are the characters in this story.

Theodore Taylor

THEODORE TAYLOR was born in North Carolina and began writing at the age of thirteen as a cub reporter for the Portsmouth, Virginia, *Evening Star*. Leaving home at seventeen to join the Washington *Daily News* as a copy boy, he worked his way toward New York City and became an NBC network sportswriter at the age of nineteen. Since then, he has been, variously, a prize-fighter manager, merchant seaman, naval officer, magazine writer, movie publicist and production assistant and documentary film maker. He has written four books for adults and four for children, including *The Cay* which has won eight awards, among them the Lewis Carroll Shelf Award, the Jane Addams Children's Book Award and the Commonwealth Club Silver Medal. Mr. Taylor and his wife and three children live in Laguna Beach, California.

M